Forever Faithful

The Legend of Seaman

SEP 2 7 2024

Copyright 2014 Phil Scriver

All rights reserved.
No part of this book may be reproduced or transmitted in any form or by any means, electronic or mechanical, including photocopying, recording, or by any other information storage and retrieval system without written permission from the author, except for inclusion of brief quotations.

ISBN-10: 1500407801
ISBN-13: 978-1500407803

Published Great Falls, Montana

Dedicated to Windsor
who we used for Seaman many years
in our festivals and reenactments.

"All of the facts about any historical event can never be known, simply because everything about it is not recorded."

> ---Stephen Ambrose
>   While floating on the Missouri River 1992

Theory: A formulation of apparent relationships or underlying principles of certain observed phenomena which have been verified to some degree.

> --Webster's Unabridged Dictionary

Contents

Chapter 1: Upper Missouri Breaks
Chapter 2: Seaman
Chapter 3: On the Marias
Chapter 4: Grampa Ames
Chapter 5: The sheepherder
Chapter 6: Charlie's Family
Chapter 7: NoDak
Chapter 8: Charlie's funeral
Chapter 9: Hiram's notebook
Chapter 10: War is hell
Chapter 11: Reunion
Chapter 12: St. Louis
Chapter 13: A mind out of control
Chapter 14: Believers
Chapter 15: Hiram's last feast
Chapter 16: Rest in peace
Chapter 17: Afterward

1 The Upper Missouri Breaks

"Hey, don't you know you are private land?"

"No," I responded carefully, "but…"

He cut me off with a menacing step forward as he said, "And I don't like you s.o.bs who so strongly insist upon your rights to public land then trample all over my private land. You damn fools leave gates open so my cattle get out and you scatter your garbage all over the place. Us landowners don't dare say a word or some of you idiots will sue us for not letting them access public land. It's about time we take matters into our own hands."

I stood there only half listening to him, but very carefully watching him and waiting for his next move. He acted like he was sparing for a fight. I hoped it would only be a verbal one, but I sure didn't like the looks of that 30-30 carbine he kept waving around and sometimes pointing in my direction. He stared at me for a minute until he decided that I was not going to argue or fight with him. I was unarmed so what choice did I have?

He visibly relaxed as he lowered the carbine and muttered to himself, but loud enough for me to make out, "Damn thing's not loaded anyway."

After a brief pause a bit of the fire rekindled as he again challenged me with, "What you doing out here, anyway?"

"Getting a few photos and a lot of exercise," as I held up my camera and gave him what I hoped he would take as a grin.

"Stupid government meddling. Even those dumb fools should have been able to see the problems they were creating when they made these breaks a national monument. They didn't even own half the land they said was a National Monument. They just don't understand how mixed up this country is with private, state and federal land. How could people be expected to keep it all straight?"

I carefully watched him, not really sure what his next move might be. But as he blew off the frustration that had been building in him the fire and fight disappeared, leaving a tired old man.

I was sure I had recognized him although it had been many years since I had last seen him. We had gone to high school together, but he had been several grades behind me. As he slumped slightly forward I smiled inwardly. Dan Ames hadn't changed a bit over the years; full of bluster, but no action.

Dan still had not figured out who I was so I introduced myself. I told him that since daylight I had been walking along the river, climbing the hills to the flat prairie above; just roaming and shooting hundreds of photos of everything. Some call the prairies empty, but I find it full of life. The White Cliffs area of the Missouri River is particularly interesting for its collection of rock formations. But to me the prairies are equally as attractive because they are so full of life. But you have to take the time to look for it.

After what would pass for an apology from Dan for his actions we sat there a while, each privately enjoying the late afternoon sun, cooled by a bit of a west breeze, the joys of living on the prairie. Eventually Dan seemed to gather enough strength to continue our conversation.

He told me most of the land we could see, over to the edge of the breaks belonged to him. Some of it had been in the family for generations. But he had added more land over the years with land he had purchased from neighbors who had given up the hard life of ranching on the Montana prairies. They either were retiring or moving on to some other line of work.

"You are fortunate to have been able to spend your life on these lands," I told Dan.

"Yeah, it's a tough way to make a living, but the life style makes it worthwhile."

"You guys that survive seem to be the ones that don't really try to get rich."

"Farming won't make you rich. A feller can only hope to make enough to live comfortable. Put a little away during the good years to carry you through the bad ones."

I showed Dan some of the photos I had taken that morning with my trusty Canon digital camera. I affectionately call it my professional point and shoot. It is considered by several photo magazines to be the top of the line point and shoot camera, but made for amateurs. I do not have enough ability to use the cameras with changeable lenses, filters and everything else the pros carry in those big bags they drag around with them all the time everywhere they go.

As we looked at the photos, I asked Dan about a strange barking-howl I had heard that morning. I grew up on these prairies about 30 miles northwest of where we sat. I had heard my share of coyotes and a few wolves, but what I had heard that morning could not be mistaken for either.

Dan studied me for a bit then asked me to describe in detail what I had heard. I told him it started almost like the bark of a dog; several high pitched barks then it seemed to transform to a long mournful howl ending in a kind of menacing growl. He wanted to know exactly where I was and how long this barking-howl went on.

I had parked my pickup that morning before daylight, where we were now sitting, on the prairie above the breaks and had made a short walk to the edge so I could get some photos of the sun coming up on the river below. As I waited the darkness was just starting to give way to the first streaks of daylight when I heard the barking-howl. It went on for about ten minutes then all was silent again.

As I retold my adventure Dan became totally captivated. When I was done he told me that several of the old timers in the area had told that same story over the years. Each one described the barking-howl the same way, and it was always just at the first beginnings of daylight. Everyone agreed it was not from a coyote or wolf or any other animal they knew of, but none of them knew what it was from.

Dan said his grandfather went to his grave believing that Seaman was out there. All of my questions trying to get more information on how he had determined it to be Seaman were met with a blank stare. I finally gave up on the subject entirely.

We talked a while longer, just stuff in general, until the sun started to cast its long afternoon shadows across the landscape before I grudgingly decided I had to leave this place and get home. As I drove along on my way home I decided to swing by and check on my sister who lived alone over on the Marias River bottom.

As I pulled into my sister's farm yard I felt an odd stillness rather than the usual bustle of livestock and other creatures. I was reminded of my days hunting in these river bottoms. During the part of the year when hunting was closed there were deer and antelope everywhere, but come fall and hunting season the stillness was deafening with not a single animal to be found.

The chickens should have been out in the yard scratching for food. I parked my pickup and walked across the yard towards the chicken house to see if I could raise any activity. As I neared the back side of the chicken pen I saw a rather large and freshly dug hole under the fence. Something wanted some chicken pretty bad to dig that big of a hole in the hard ground.

As I walked around the area I thought I saw a few large tracks in the dust. They could have been made by a mountain lion. I retraced my steps over to my sister's house. I was curious to see what kind of a story I would hear from her.

"I see your damn dog got into the chicken house again."

"Misty hasn't been able to get in there since you fixed her hole under the wire."

"Well something sure got in there. That hole she had under the wire is twice as big as it was before."

"She is a big dog and can take care of herself, but something has been out in the yard for several nights that really has her spooked. She won't go out at all after dark."

"Have you seen or heard anything?"

"No."

"Weren't your dogs going crazy over the smells or the noises out there?"

You know Misty isn't the bravest creature on earth; and Shelty was protecting her. I don't think either one made much noise. They knew something was out there but neither one was going to venture out to see what it was."

"Yeah I forgot, your two cow dogs that are both afraid of cattle."

"Now don't start in on my dogs again. You know they are good company for me."

"I suppose so. I don't know why you stay out here alone. You have either leased or sold all the land except for a few acres the house sits on. The only livestock you have is a few chickens. You have even quit growing a garden. Why don't you sell what you have left and move to town?"

"Oh I don't know. I guess I have always lived here and never had any troubles til now. I enjoy the quiet our here. All those people in town would drive me crazy."

"Oh my, Fort Benton is so huge! Try Billings or Denver sometime if you want to talk about crowds of people."

"No thanks; I'll stay here with my two brave dogs and the chickens."

"Well, I'll go out and have a closer look around; see if I can find some tracks or if any chickens have been killed."

I left my sister busily working away at something in the kitchen and strolled out across the yard towards the chicken house. As I got closer I realized things were strangely quite everywhere in the yard. Something had definitely been out here not very long ago and put a big scare into everything. As I looked closer at the chicken house and pen I saw enough evidence that I knew I had to get my camera to get some photos of what I would find from a close examination of the area. I returned to the house to let my sister know what was going on.

"Hey, I'm sorry I accused your dumb dog of chasing chickens."

"I wish you would quit picking on Misty. She never did anything to you."

"I found tracks around the chicken yard that look to me could be mountain lion. But I've never seen mountain lion this far out on the prairie. I also saw some other tracks. They were pretty big to be coyote tracks or from your darling mongrel, Misty. There were several piles of feathers, but it didn't look like any of the chickens had been killed since I couldn't find any blood."

"That's good. They are almost big enough to butcher. I would hate to lose the meat."

"It almost looks like a mountain lion got into the yard, but something scared it off before it could catch any of the chickens."

"Do you really think it was a mountain lion way out here?"

"I'm not sure. I am going to do some further checking though. I want to get a photo of those tracks and see if I can find out for sure what made them."

"Do you think there is any point in watching the yard for the next few nights? With your new night vision scope you might see something, and I know you have been anxious to use it."

"Yeah, but first I want to get those tracks checked out. I want to know what we may be up against. I'm going to see if I can get some photos of those tracks and take them in to the Fish and Game. They might be able to tell me what kind of animal made them."

"After you take some photos just upload them to my computer and we can send them by email to the

Fish and Game. They can start looking at them while you are on your way to town."

"I'll get my camera and get out there before the wind blows those tracks away."

I understood why she was still living on the old ranch, even if it had become pretty rundown. This was the family homestead where we were all raised and she did not deal well with crowds. She had never learned to like to be around groups of people so a half dozen people were a crowd to her. She definitely liked her solitude.

My sister wasn't the handiest person and home repairs were well beyond her capabilities. The only time any maintenance got done was when I, or one of the other members of the extended family, came out and did it. That didn't happen very often since they were all busy trying to make a living on their own modest-sized dryland farms. Consequently whenever I came out, even if only for a quick stop, I made notes of what needed to be repaired or replaced. If she had any urgent fixes that needed to be done I could usually take some time for them. Most of the time small jobs were easy enough to get done, but today I didn't have enough daylight to do anything other than take some photos of the tracks and get back on the road.

I lived in town about two hours away, but it seemed as though I spent most of my time traveling to do research or interview people. Even writing simple fiction demanded many hours of travel and research.

I got home late that night. After getting several good photos of the different tracks around the chicken house, I downloaded them to my sister's computer then emailed a set to the Fish and Game.

The next day as I dumped the photos from my trip through the breaks onto my computer "Lewis and Clark" entered my thoughts again. How could it possibly have been Seaman I had heard howling? I could make absolutely no sense of the whole thing. But I had heard something that definitely was not a coyote or wolf.

I couldn't shake the thought of Seaman so I gave in and told myself that I would at least spend some time re-reading the Expedition journals. Maybe something in them or some later correspondence from or to Meriwether Lewis would shed some light on the matter. I knew there had been some research done on Seaman to try to find out if he had even made it all the way back to St. Louis with the Expedition. However nothing conclusive had ever been found so everything was just theories.

With that promise made to myself I spent the rest of the day catching up on several other details that I had set aside so I could take my trip to the Missouri River breaks.

I awoke the following morning to a bright and sunny day that just begged me to forget everything else and get out on the prairies to enjoy life. Alas, I could not forsake the promise I made. Seaman was waiting. After breakfast I begrudgingly took my cup of coffee down to my office in the basement to get started.

2 Seaman

The day, July 16, marked the start of my search for Seaman. I picked volume 2 of the Journals of the Lewis and Clark Expedition, edited by Dr. Gary Moulton from my bookshelf and the journey began. My task was to see everything that was written in the Expedition's journals about the dog. As I remembered from past readings there wasn't very much written about him, but I had to be sure what had been said.

Lewis left Washington and went to Philadelphia to gather supplies for the modest-sized military unit he was to put together to explore the lands from St. Louis to the Pacific Ocean. They were to travel up the Missouri River to its headwaters then make a short portage to the headwaters of the Columbia River. From there the Expedition would follow that river to the Pacific.

Lewis would also use his time in Philadelphia studying under the watchful eyes of several of the best scientists and scholars in America.

When he had completed his tasks in Philadelphia Lewis returned to Washington for final instructions from Jefferson. After the 4th of July Lewis departed Washington bound for Pittsburgh where his storehouse of supplies had been shipped. At Pittsburgh he ordered a keelboat built to his specifications. He would use the keelboat to haul his supplies down the Ohio River to the Mississippi River and on to winter quarters at St. Louis.

While his boat was being built Lewis busied himself inventorying and repacking the supplies and otherwise making ready for his "darling tour" across the continent. He also recruited a small crew to help him with the boat. If they met his expectations they would continue on as part of the exploring party.

With the work all done Lewis found he had time on his hands so he wandered the area re-acquainting himself with places he remembered from time spent here in the early days of his military career. In some of his wanderings he met a man who sold him a large black dog. Lewis would later relate in his Journal he paid the man $20 for the Newfoundland he named Seaman.

Almost as soon as they laid eyes on each other a strong bond seemed to form between Lewis and Seaman that would require the purchase to be made. The man saw this and took full advantage of the situation by setting a very high price then refusing to submit to any bargaining. Lewis agreed although it represented two months of his Army pay.

As a kid growing up in the Virginia country and later as he rambled across the frontiers of the Carolinas and Georgia, Lewis always had dogs around. They were just a part of his life. But since the time he joined the Army there hadn't been any. He felt an emptiness in his life because of it. Lewis was determined to fill that void before he faced the biggest challenge of his life. He had to have a companion.

Finally, by the end of August the boat was ready. In the early hours of the 30th Lewis and his crew steered the keelboat into the main current of the Ohio River and they were on their way. It had almost been an unbearable wait while the boat was being built, but now that was all behind him. He was free from the bonds of civilization.

With his companion, Seaman, by his side he was ready for the adventures ahead. The excitement of adventure in the unknown quickly gave way to the work of navigating the keelboat down the river that was so low on water they constantly ran aground on unseen sandbars. It was slow going, but according to his journal entries a certain amount of joy for the long-awaited adventure remained.

As I perused the journal writings of Captain Lewis that chronicled his trip down the Ohio River he wrote very little about his new dog. Lewis had departed Pittsburgh on August 31, 1803, but it wasn't until September 11th that he mentioned Seaman. On the 11th and again on the 14th Lewis noted he had Seaman catching squirrels that were swimming across the river. He remarked this was a common occurrence.

The next mention of Seaman was on November 16. Here we see for the first time the attachment that is developing between Lewis and his dog. Lewis wrote, "One of the Shawnees a respectable looking Indian offered me three beaver skins for my dog with which he appeared much pleased. (This was somewhat less than what Lewis had paid in Pittsburgh for Seaman). The dog was a Newfoundland breed one that I prized much for his docility and qualifications generally for my journey and of course there was no bargain. I had given $20 for this dog myself."

Lewis is silent about Seaman until late April 25, 1805 when he laments, "My dog had been absent during the last night and I was fearful we had lost him altogether, however much to my satisfaction he joined us at 8 o'clock this morning."

More trouble befell Seaman on May 19th. Lewis wrote, "One of the party wounded a beaver and my dog as usual swam in to catch it. The beaver bit him through the hind leg and cut the artery. It was great difficulty that I could stop the blood. I fear it will yet prove fatal to him."

The evening of May 28th was a busy time. Lewis wrote, "last night we were alarmed by a large buffalo bull which swam over from the opposite shore and coming alongside the white pirogue climbed over it to land. He then alarmed ran up the bank in full speed directly toward the fires and within 18 inches of the heads of some of the men as they lay yet sleeping before the sentinel could alarm him or make him change directions. He now took his direction immediately towards our lodge. When he came near my dog saved us by causing him to change his direction to the right and he was soon out of sight."

A careful examination of the camp the next morning showed how close the buffalo came to the men. It had broken York's rifle, also broke the spindle & pivot (on one of the oars) and shattered the stock of one of the blunder buses on board the pirogue.

Seaman proved his value as a guard dog again on June 19 at the Lower Portage Camp near the Great Falls. Lewis' journal entry shows, ""after dark my dog barked very much and seemed extremely uneasy which was unusual with him. I ordered the sgt. of the guard to reconnoiter with two men thinking it possible some Indians might be about to pay us a visit or perhaps a white bear. He returned soon after and reported that he believed the dog had been baying a buffalo which had attempted to swim the river just above our camp but had been beaten down stream by the current and landed below our camp and run off."

Another interesting entry from Lewis' journal dated April 11, 1806 shows how total his attachment for Seaman had become. He wrote, "Three of this same tribe of villans the Wahclellars stole my dog this evening and took him towards their village. I was shortly afterwards informed of this transaction by an Indian who spoke the Clatsop language and sent three men in pursuit of the thieves with orders if they made the least resistance or difficulty in surrendering the dog to fire on them. They overtook the fellows or rather came in sight of them at the distance of about 2 miles.

The Indians on discovering the party in pursuit of them left the dog and fled."

Most of the rest of the journal entries that mention Seaman relate to his abilities to catch game animals and birds, although Lewis does brag a bit about Seaman's intelligence on August 17, 1805. The last entry that can be found about the dog was made on July 15, 1806 when Lewis' party was at the Great Falls of the Missouri. He recorded, "the mosquitos continue to infest us in such manner we can scarcely exist. My dog even howls with the torture he experiences from them."

After completing my search of the Expedition's written records I did a quick summary of what I had learned. Lewis bought a dog in Pittsburgh for $20, which was a high price to pay. A bond developed between the dog and Lewis that was so strong that Lewis potentially put the entire Expedition in jeopardy to get Seaman's return when Indians stole him. Seaman was last heard from when the Expedition was barely half way back to St. Louis from the Pacific Ocean.

If such a strong bond had actually been formed, there must be more to the story. I determined that I had to find out.

I was on a roll. After completing my search for references to Seaman in the journals written by Lewis and Clark, I continued my attack. I turned to the few references I found on the internet. What little fact I found there had to be validated by other sources.

I knew the national Lewis and Clark organization published a quarterly magazine that was highly regarded in historical circles. An examination of past issues of that publication produced results that validated most of what I had found earlier on the internet.

Although Seaman is talked about by both Lewis and Clark in their journals, there are only about two dozen comments made during the entire three years of the expedition. Frequently there were long periods of time Seaman is not mentioned. But every mention sounded like it was representative of common activities that don't need daily comment. Most people realize he is not gone during the times he is not written about. One of these periods is eight months long. The author of one article I read reasoned that given all these periods of silence, often lasting several months, the fact we hear nothing about the dog from mid-July 1806 until the expedition is back in St. Louis in late September doesn't mean anything. There was simply nothing of importance going on that involved Seaman, so there was no reason to mention him in the writings. If the dog had not completed the trip the Captains would have told the story in the journals.

Since journal keepers don't necessarily write about the common events, Seaman appears to get mentioned only when something different or unusual happens. The buffalo coming into camp is a good example. Seaman and his activity around camp was a common event as he followed the group trudging along their route to the ocean.

A book written by Timothy Alden in 1814 was a collection of epitaphs and inscriptions. He included one entry about a dog collar in an Alexandria, Virginia museum. He wrote, "The greatest traveler of my species. My name is SEAMAN, the dog of Captain Meriwether Lewis, whom I accompanied to the Pacifick Ocean through the interior of the continent of North America."

A note in the book about the collar said, "The foregoing was copied from the collar, in the Alexandria Museum, which the late Gov. Lewis' dog wore after his return from the western coast of America. The fidelity and attachment of this animal were remarkable. After the melancholy exit of Gov. Lewis, his dog would not depart for a moment from his lifeless remains; and when they were deposited in the earth no gentle means could draw him from the spot of interment. He refused to take every kind of food, which was offered him, and actually pined away and died with grief upon his master's grave."

Correspondence from the museum to Captain Clark shows it was probably Clark who gave the collar to the museum.

Because the actual collar and most of the museum relics burned in an 1871 fire Seaman's fate can't be definitely proven. But the article concludes the fate of Seaman must have been as the 1814 book note says. No additional material has been found to prove or indicate otherwise.

After I finished my research on what facts were known about Lewis' dog I felt unsatisfied. In my mind I pictured a place where Seaman had been buried or at least some sort of a marker had been erected that told for certain the end of Seaman's story.

I remembered the story of Shep, a sheepherder's dog in the Fort Benton area. His master had died. When his body was brought to Fort Benton for shipment back east on the train for burial, Shep followed. For several years Shep met every train coming into the small town, hoping his master was returning. Eventually age got the upper hand and Shep passed onto his maker.

During his life in Fort Benton waiting for his master's return, Shep had become famous. Even though he refused most attempts of people trying to befriend him, everyone in town turned out for his funeral just as they would have done for a person of importance. His grave on a hillside overlooking the train depot is still marked by a large memorial.

I could find no mention of any marker or monument or grave for Seaman. I searched the internet to no avail.

I put that research aside, at least temporarily, in favor of starting a new search. Lewis had written that he prized Seaman for his qualifications in general, but didn't elaborate. What qualities could Lewis have been talking about? I decided that I needed to know more about the Newfoundland breed of dogs. An internet search provided an interesting story. I read details from numerous websites. These included the Newfoundland Club of America, Gentle Newfoundland Dogs and Vet Street. There was also a small book on the North American Newfoundland Club website that was particularly interesting. Each one seemed to have different ideas about the breed's history, but all generally agreed to the dogs' disposition and traits.

It appears there are two parts to the Newfoundland history, ancient and modern. The ancient history goes back at least until the days of the Vikings in Eastern Canada. This part of the history says the Newfoundland is a cross between the Norse Bear Dog and some combination of several other large breeds from Europe. This dog was referred to as being called Hero Dogs. Their actual time and place of origin is unknown, but it widely considered a very old breed.

The modern dog originated in Newfoundland and was probably a cross between the smaller St. John Dog and the now extinct Black Wolf. The name Newfoundland was first used for this breed in 1775. The breed was by then a very large work dog. It was commonly used to work in harness pulling wagons. According to the North American Newfoundland Club website they hauled their loads over great distances with no human in charge. When they reached their destination and the load was emptied they would return to where they came on their own.

The Newfoundland is called a gentle giant dog because of its size and temperament. Today 170-180 pounds is common while two centuries ago 150-160 pounds was more the average. Their web feet make them strong swimmers with a natural instinct to rescue people in the water. These dogs form close bonds with people, in fact they do not seem to do well in a solitary life. There are many accounts of Newfoundlands being devoted to their owners and of many lives being saved by them.

I have heard over the years that the early Newfoundland dogs were much smaller than they are today. After reading about these dogs I wonder if these people might have been thinking of the St. John Dog by mistake. The work these dogs were doing at the time of the Lewis and Clark Expedition was not that of a small dog unless there were working in teams like sled dogs do. I saw no reports of them doing so.

The entire history of the evolution of the Newfoundland breed is quite conflicted by many artists, and even knowledgeable animal owners, who used wrong names for their breed of dogs. This was particularly true in earlier times when dog breeders didn't keep definitive records. The end result is that the history is more speculative than factual.

As I read about these Newfoundland dogs my mind flashed to Lewis and Clark Expedition member Patrick Gass' book about the journey. In it he has a drawing of a grizzly bear that chased a man up a tree. The bear looks much more like a large dog than a bear. Maybe he used Seaman for his model when he drew the picture. I also thought about Lewis' comments that while the men were making a side trip to visit the Spirit Mound, Seaman became too hot and tired to travel on so they sent him back to the creek to cool off. Nobody went with him.

There were other details mentioned in the journals that caught my attention. Lewis said that Seaman was able to chase down the fleet antelope during late winter at Fort Mandan. He compared Seaman's method of chase to that of a single wolf rather than how several coyotes would have accomplished the task. This might have been a telltale sign of his wolf ancestors. Lewis also gave the impression that a large dog was more successful guarding camp from invading buffalo or grizzly bear.

I was getting a fairly good picture of what Captain Lewis' dog was. But there were a few choice words I had come across in my reading that I decided to check out a little bit further. I had not seen words like acumen, sagacity, astute, valor, discerning or shrewd applied to a dog before. These are terms normally used to describe a person. However, Lewis had referred to his dog's "segacity" being an object of admiration for the Shoshones in the late summer of 1805. Since I am still old school in some ways I grabbed my oversized and well-worn dictionary and commenced reading. I discovered that Lewis was simply saying that his dog was very intelligent.

The picture I finally developed in my mind is of a very large dog, 160-170 pounds, who is at home on land or in the water. He is quite a fast runner and a strong swimmer. This dog is docile and doesn't waste a lot of energy running aimlessly about on the scent trail of animals long gone. He wanted the closeness of people, but has formed a particularly close bond with Lewis. He did his part on the journey by guarding camp at night, in particular keeping large animals such as bears, buffalo and wolves at bay. Small animals that ventured a little too close or waited a bit too long before trying to escape frequently fell victim to Seaman's jaws. He often showed his retriever ancestry and caught large game animals such as antelope and deer that one of the hunters wounded. Seaman was friendly to all the members of the Expedition and never missed a chance for a pat or scratch behind the ears from any of them. But he was unmistakably Lewis' dog.

If Seaman was actually a dog like I have developed in my mind, then his death "with grief upon his master's grave" as was suggested by Alden could be a reasonable conclusion to be drawn.

3 On the Marias

I was satisfied that I had found out everything I was going to about Seaman. The theories dating back to 1814 about his death were sensible. I decided to set Seaman aside and get on with one of my several other projects that had the prospects of producing some much needed income. It is fun to run around the country, but the mundane jobs seem to be what pays the bills.

I occupied myself the next day looking really busy, but my heart wasn't into any of these new projects. I couldn't clear my head of that bark-howl I had heard that early morning in the Missouri River breaks.

I had a habit when things weren't going particularly well, I would pause and check my email. I don't really know when or why I acquired this habit since all I ever got was spam, with occasional invitations to join some online group discussion that was of absolutely no interest to me. But today a real email jumped out at me.

The Fish and Game responded to my inquiry on the photos of the tracks I had taken around my sister's chicken house. They told me there definitely had been a mountain lion there, but it had been chased off by a wolf. That was quite unusual, but not unheard of.

That was all the excuse I needed to set aside my projects that weren't going anywhere anyway. I told myself that I needed to get out to my sister's place and see if the mountain lion had decided to wander on. A phone call would not help matters since she would just tell me that she and the dogs were staying in the house until the dogs decided they could venture out. With those two cowardly dogs, who knows how long that would be.

I determined I would make a trip out to my sister's place the next morning. I needed to try to find out about the mountain lion and if she also had a wolf or wolves in the area. I grabbed my large duffel bag and packed into it my night vision scope and extra rounds of ammunition for my 30-06 rifle that was older than me. It kicked like a mule, but it still shot true. I also packed my camera bag with several extra boxes of batteries and an extra flash drive to store my photos on. My duffel bag, 30-06 rifle, two tripods for my camera and my .22 pistol were stowed into the cab of my pickup so I would be ready to go in the morning.

I very seldom took my rifle or pistol with me on my travels, but with the threat of encountering mountain lions and wolves I figured I better have both. I might need to try to scare something off. I surely couldn't depend upon hitting what I aimed at in a hurried situation since I shot these weapons so seldom any more. In days gone by many deer, antelope and elk had fallen prey to my 30-06, but that was a long time ago. Any more I did most of my shooting with my Canon digital camera.

I made a quick phone call to the Fish and Game primarily to acknowledge their email, but I also wanted to make an appointment to stop and talk further with them about these animals running around my sister's place. Had something happened to all of a sudden make her farm attractive for animals that didn't normally live in that area? I couldn't imagine what that might be, but several kinds of animals we now think of as living in the mountains are becoming more common further out onto the prairies. People are saying it is because of the increased numbers of several species of animals that need space to live. That probably is true since we never had anything but maybe a few deer and antelope around the place when I was a kid growing up there.

The next morning I left as the first shades of light were just starting to make themselves known in the morning sky; since it was early August that meant about 4:30 a.m. I was in for a long day, but I wanted to get the Fish and Game office early so we would have all day to check out the tracks I had photographed.

After a quick trip to Fort Benton, I pulled in to the Fish and Game parking lot, fully expecting a long wait until someone showed up. Although the field biologist I had talked with yesterday had promised to be there by the time I arrived, any time after 5:00 a.m., I was skeptical. Most people simply don't like early mornings, particularly state and federal employees who have an aversion to work any time other than 8:00 to 5:00.

As soon as I turned off the pickup's engine the door to the front entrance to the building opened and a young-looking man stepped out. I climbed out of the pickup and was met by a greeting I thought was much too cheery to be sincere.

"Good morning. I am Roy Young the field biologist for the Fish and Game. You talked with me yesterday about some lion tracks."

I responded with my usual direct, "Yes you did. I'm glad to see you although I must admit I am surprised to see you this early."

"I told you I would be here."

"Yeah, I know, but I have become skeptical, I guess."

"I understand. Most people don't like early mornings except farmers in the Spring when they are first getting into their fields for the year."

"I guess I've learned over the years to deal with whatever it takes to get the job done."

"I've got my laptop just in case we needed to compare some tracks; if you want we can head out for your sister's place now. I would like to get a good look at the situation before the tracks get any more disturbed."

We crawled back into our pickups and headed out for the Marias. It was only a 30 minute trip, mostly on pavement. I led since Roy wasn't sure he knew which place was my sister's.

My sister met us at the gate into her yard. Her two not-so-brave dogs hung close behind her. After the hellos she told us she had kept the dogs away from the chicken house so they didn't mess up the tracks we had photographed. She also told us they hadn't seen or heard anything unusual since the events a few nights ago.

Roy and I walked over to the chicken house while my sister took her dogs back inside the house. I showed Roy the tracks I had seen and where a hole had been dug under the fence. He carefully examined the area then started circling the entire yard. Each circle got larger as he continued walking and examining the ground to find tracks that would show where the animals had come from and went to when they left the area. I watched as he worked until he was finally satisfied he had seen everything.

As he walked up to me he said, "Looks to me there was a young male mountain lion that came visiting a few nights ago. He got scared off before he got anything to eat, so he probably won't be back."

"Yeah, that's about what I thought."

"The lion tracks are plain. He came up from the river to the yard. Whatever scared him off chased him back down to the trees along the river."

"I guess I'm not much of a tracker. I only saw the tracks in the yard, so I wasn't sure, but that makes sense. He would be safe once he could get up a tree."

Roy was warming to the job. We walked around the yard and he showed me the tracks where the lion had come up from the river. He could tell by the relationship of the front and rear feet tracks that it was moving slowly, like it was sneaking up on its prey. He then showed me where the lion traveled when he was scared away from the chicken house. The tracks he left as he sought the safety of the trees showed he was in full flight. Mixed in with this set of tracks were some made by a different animal.

We followed these tracks backwards from the edge of the yard back to the chicken house and the large hole under the fence.

"This is where I first found these other tracks," Roy said. "It's funny but I could not find any tracks to show me where the guy came from. Wolves are not particularly good about hiding their tracks, but this one just seems to appear here."

"These are definitely too big for any coyote tracks I have ever seen or any dogs either," I said more to myself that anyone else.

We bent down to carefully examine the tracks around the chicken house. The mountain lion tracks were obviously different from the others.

Roy pointed to the other set of tracks, "Some of the big dogs can have tracks almost as large as wolf tracks. But dog tracks tend to be a little longer than they are wide and the front are bigger that the rear."

"These tracks look to be square shaped to me and the front and rear are about the same size. That's how I remember wolf tracks to be."

Roy agreed, "Although some of the large dogs make tracks that are impossible to distinguish from wolf tracks. In this ground we can't really get a full track like we could in the mud." He went on to say, "It's odd too, that the inside of these tracks are not clear. Compared to the lion tracks these look fuzzier."

"I just thought that was from the wind blowing the dust around and filling in the tracks."

"That's probably true for part of the difference, but if so why wouldn't the wind do the same thing to the lion tracks?"

"Yeah, you're right about that."

"Let's follow these tracks down to the trees on the river again so we can get a better look at them while these animals were on the move. It will give us a better comparison of front and rear tracks."

Several times Roy stopped and knelt down to carefully study the tracks as we made our way the few hundred yards to the river.

"Look here" Roy almost shouted as he excitedly pointed to the ground just ahead, both our friends here went sliding in the mud when they tried to turn too quick to avoid falling over the edge of this bank into the river."

"These tracks are too smeared for me to tell anything," I announced after a brief examination.

"Yeah," Roy agreed, "we can't tell what made them; just that something in a big hurry almost fell over the edge here and that something else was chasing it. There are definitely two different sets of tracks."

"Look, over there on that tree," We said at the same time, "Looks like claw marks to me."

"Hey, they go all the way up to that big limb, about fifteen feet up," Roy observed.

"Our lion spent some time in that tree; probably safely out of reach of whatever was chasing him."

After a few more minutes looking around we could not find anything else to help us put the final pieces of the puzzle together. The tracks seemed to stop at the tree. We lost them in the leaves and brush.

"Well I think we have found everything we're going to find down here. We may as well head back."

"Yeah, I'm going to get some more photos of these tracks down here and where the lion climbed that tree."

"I'll leave you to it. The state pays me to work, not just sit around shooting the bull."

"Okay and thanks. I would never have found these tracks down here or the claw marks."

"Well that's what they pay me the big bucks for."

"I guess I can tell my sister it is safe to let her dogs out again."

"Yeah, I'm sure these critters are long gone by now. They won't be back any time soon."

I watched as Roy turned his pickup down the driveway to the highway. After scraping a little dried mud off my shoes I went into my sister's house to relate what we had discovered.

As I drove back home I reviewed our finding. Everything made sense to me except what treed that mountain lion. Wolves don't normally chase lions and tree them. But if those weren't wolf tracks, what were they? Where did those tracks come from before we found them at the Chicken house? Where did they go after they left the tree the lion had been in? The mountain lion problem was resolved, but what had treed him? That question would not go away. I finally agreed with myself that I would quit thinking about that question for now. I would come back to it later. First I wanted to find more about that mysterious bark-howl.

By the time I reached home I had developed a plan of action to try to put this barking-howl situation to rest. First I would get in contact with Dan Ames again and try to get some detailed information and see why his grandfather was so sure he had heard Seaman.

The next morning after breakfast I headed downstairs to my office with a fresh cup of coffee in hand. I called Dan Ames and arranged to go out to his place and talk with him. I had to find out why his grandfather was so sure what he had heard those many years ago was Seaman.

It was arranged for me to see Dan at the end of the week. They still had about four, maybe five, days of harvest work left to get finished. Nothing except maybe death or rain holds up harvest on a Montana wheat farm. A late summer hail storm, heavy rains, or high winds will quickly destroy a year's work. There are just too many things that can happen to ruin an entire crop so when the wheat is ripe you harvest it and don't leave anything to chance.

I spent the rest of the week taking care of details I had put aside. I could feel myself getting absorbed in a strange tale. I knew that once I got caught up in the Seaman business it might be a long time before things returned to normal in my life.

Although time dragged so minutes became hours, I worked through a considerable list of projects I was determined to finish before I did anything else.

4
Grampa Ames

The day for my meeting out at Dan Ames place in the Missouri River breaks finally arrived. I had loaded my gear the night before so I could get an early start. It was a three hour drive out to Dan's place out on the prairie above the Eagle Creek breaks south of Big Sandy. I wanted to take the opportunity to enjoy the sunrise and early morning calm on the prairie. I intended to get out to Dan's as early as possible. I remembered when we were still kids in school he was not the most dependable person as far as being on time for appointments. During my visits with the Fish and Game people in Fort Benton about the tracks around my sister's place I found that Dan's dependability hadn't improved much over the years. If I let much daylight pass he may just as likely as not get busy on something else and totally forget about our meeting. I didn't know how early a riser he was, but I wasn't taking any chances. For some strange reason this situation had become too important to me to let anything get in its way.

I pulled into the yard at the Ames farm at 7:30 am. To the sound of several dogs barking as if they dared me to step out of my pickup and face them. I pulled up to the fence around the house yard and calmly walked over to the gate, opened it, and headed up the walk to the front door. Three dogs quickly cut me off, barking their heads off, with tails wagging a mile a minute. I thought, typical Dan Ames, all bark and no bite.

"I see you found the place okay."

"Yeah, I even surprised myself how well I remembered the area. Your directions were fine."

"Come on in, the coffee pot's on. If you would have been here any earlier I would still have been in bed."

"Well I wasn't sure how early you would be getting up, so I got here early enough that I could enjoy the sunrise. And I wasn't taking any chances of you getting busy on something else before I got here."

"Oh, no chance of that now harvest is done. This Seaman legend and my grandfather are too important for me to miss out."

"That's definitely good to hear since it seems to be consuming me too."

"Let's go inside and get some of that coffee, no use standing out here when we can sit down and be comfortable in the house."

I followed Dan into the kitchen and sat at the table he motioned me to. While he poured two cups of coffee and brought them to the table I pulled out my notebook and pen. I had tried using various kinds of recorders for these interviews, but they never seemed to work for me as well as my good old fashioned paper and pencil.

As he sat down Dan asked, "Now what's got you all fired up about my grandfather and the Seaman legend?"

"I must admit that I hadn't given Seaman much thought as I studied Lewis and Clark over the years. I knew his basic story on the Expedition and naturally assumed he returned to St. Louis with the rest of the crew. Lewis didn't write much about him in his journals, so I wasn't too concerned. I figured if something would have happened to him, Lewis would have said so."

"So what changed our mind?"

"That morning out on the river when I heard that howling then, later, your remarks about your grandfather."

"What, that wolf howl?"

I smiled and said, "Come now, we both know I didn't hear a wolf. I know what a wolf howl sounds like and I know what I heard wasn't any wolf."

"Okay, okay you caught me."

"You know I didn't describe a wolf, or coyote either, when I told you what I heard. And I know from your response you had heard that description before."

"Yes I have. Okay, no more games?"

"Good. I am too engrossed in this to get caught up in games. It's going to take too much time and effort to find out the real details. I don't want to have to sift through a bunch of games and garbage purposely added too."

"All right here is what I know. I personally have never heard the bark-howl you described to me and neither did my father. However my grandfather heard it several times over the years and described it to me using almost the exact words you did."

"I suspected that was the case when I saw your reaction that day over by the river."

"My grandfather, Jacob Ames, was raised in Iowa. He homesteaded here in 1910. In fact I still own his homestead."

We sat there most of the morning drinking coffee as Dan continued filling in all the details he knew about his grandfather, the bark-howl, Seaman and several friends and acquaintances of his grandfather. Most of them were Army buddies and, like him, veterans of the Spanish American War. When his grandfather came to this part of Montana he was a young man. He spent the rest of his life on his beloved ranch even after his wife passed on and left him alone.

One of his kids stayed on the farm. He married and built his home on neighboring property several miles away. That was Dan's father, Henry, and Dan now lived on the place his father had built. His grandfather's homestead was just a couple miles away down on Eagle Creek near its mouth on the Missouri River. Dan had eventually torn down what remained of the few buildings that had been standing and cleaned up the property that had become basically a pile of junk. Dan's father had already moved most everything of value up to the home place before he had a stroke and died at an early age. Out in this country there was no such thing as emergency help in the late '50s. He had been dead for several hours before anyone found him.

Dan had been very reluctant in cleaning up the remains of his grandfather's homestead at the "request" of the Bureau of Land Management, who managed this area of the Missouri River. They said that it would make the landscape more appealing to visitors who were floating through the Missouri Breaks National Monument. It was one of the locations that guides liked because they could point it out and tell some history of the area. They wanted it to be pristine like it was when the Lewis and Clark Expedition camped here on May 31, 1805.

I suspect that they pressured him a lot more than he told me. His nature was that he dug in his heels and resisted when the "government" came in telling him what to do on his private property. Since it was his land he could do or not do whatever he wanted and the government couldn't dictate to him like they were trying to do. That is probably why he got to be so opposed to the national monument and government intervention. It is also probably why he threatened me when he first saw me several weeks earlier.

The rest of Dan's aunts and uncles scattered across the country in pursuit of their own lives and dreams, only occasionally returning to their birthplace for short visits when they could fit them into family plans.

Dan continued his narrative about Seaman. During the fifty years Jacob Ames had lived on his river homestead, he had heard the bark-howl numerous times. It seemed to go in cycles. For a week or so he would hear it three or four times then it would disappear, not to be heard again for years.

Jacob had talked about it to others who lived in this area. Some people heard it, but most never did. Very seldom did anyone who lived back off the river ever hear the bark. It was most frequently heard for about the first twenty years Jacob lived on the river then it went away and was last heard in the early 1950s. At that time most everyone that heard it thought it was a bit odd, but agreed it had to be a wolf. What else could it be? There were only two or three that thought otherwise. They didn't know what it was, but they refused to even seriously consider it might have been a wolf or coyote.

Jacob and an old sheepherder who lived farther east in the south end of the Bear Paws and ran sheep in the Haystack Butte and Tiger Butte area were both convinced they were listening to Lewis' dog Seaman calling for his master. They both knew the ancient Indian legends about Spirit Mound.

When I heard the bark-howl a few weeks earlier was the first time it had been reported since those days in the early '50s.

Dan didn't say anything further about how his grandfather knew it was Seaman he heard. All that his grandfather said was he knew it was him because the legend of Spirit Mound told him so. He would end the discussion with, "Sometimes things are so powerful a person just has to quit trying to figure it out and have faith."

Dan wrapped up the session by telling me that all the people his grandfather knew that had heard the bark-howl were dead except possibly one of the old sheepherders. The last Dan had heard, which was several years ago, he was in an assisted living place either in Montana or possibly in Idaho.

We had talked all morning. At Dan's insistence we had a quick lunch then jumped onto 4-wheelers for a ride down to the river to have a look around. I grabbed my camera; a person never knows when a photo op will happen.

Dan gave me a tour of the river homestead and the breaks in general for a couple of miles along the river in each direction. He told me that he could never make very much out of his grandfather's story, but if I saw the territory we had been talking about maybe it would help me in my efforts.

He showed me the hill his grandfather most often said the bark-howl came from. Although it was always heard early in the morning when it was still dark out, this was his best calculation as to where it came from.

I knew some of these farmers were quite accurate on identifying where sounds came from at night. I remember when I was a kid of eight or nine out on the farm. There was a big old male cat that ran around the countryside. He would kill any kittens he could find. One night my father heard a cat meowing.

We had a mother cat that had recently given birth to a litter of five kittens so he grabbed his .22 rifle and shot into the night in the direction of the meow. The next morning Dad found a dead cat about 150 yards away from the house over by the haystacks.

At Dan's insistence we climbed the hill and looked around. I don't know what he thought we would find, but to my surprise this was the same place I had heard the bark-howl come from. When I told Dan about it he was skeptical. His mood changed to show he thought I was either poking fun at him or patronizing him. But when we found the tracks I had made a few days earlier while I was examining the area his friendly mood immediately returned. There was a place where I had to do a controlled slide across a cliff face to get from where I had been that night over to this hill.

We spent most of the afternoon in the breaks and I took several hundred photos. Thanks to the miracles of digital photography I could take all I wanted to be sure and get the shots I was after. All the excess ones could simply be deleted. We finally made our way back to Dan's place and I headed home.

I would need to spend a few days compiling my notes and reviewing photos before I hit the trail again to track down the old sheepherder and go talk with him. While Montana and Idaho together are a large territory, there are not too many towns that have retirement homes for me to make contact with. A few hours on the phone should do the trick.

But finding him may prove to be the easy part. Getting to where he was living may take longer. It's a big country and the only way to get from one place to another is by car. That takes time. With any luck he would still be mentally alert enough to carry on a conversation that both he and I could understand. He was getting up there in years, but I have seen several people that were almost a hundred years old who were still in full control of their mental state.

5 The Sheepherder

It was a quite a task, but I finally tracked down Dan's sheepherder. When we had talked earlier he could not remember the old guy's name. All he could remember was everyone called him "Crazy Charlie" but Dan didn't think that was his real name. He didn't really know what ever happened to him either. Some stories said he was still somewhere in Montana while others said he went back to Iowa where he grew up. Others were positive he had died, but his burial location was unknown. The only other information Dan could give me was that when Crazy Charlie left Meechum's place he said he was going down to the southern Idaho desert country where it was warmer in the winters.

I started calling retirement homes, but my search efforts were stymied because I didn't think it would be appropriate to ask for Crazy Charlie, so I limited it to Charlie the sheepherder. Finally, in my frustrations of not getting any response, yes or no, from anyone I asked for Crazy Charlie. To my surprise this brought an immediate positive response. It seemed like they all knew Crazy Charlie. He had spent time in retirement homes all over the state. He just couldn't seem to overcome his wanderlust. I finally caught up with him at the Old Soldier's Home in Columbia Falls. So I made arrangements to go see him. That would be two weeks after my visit with Dan at his place out on Eagle Creek.

I timed my meeting with Crazy Charlie to be mid-morning as the nurses at the Old Soldiers home suggested. They said mid-morning was when he was at his best. By noon he would need to eat then take an afternoon nap before having supper. Then it was off to bed for the night.

When I sat down with him he seemed spry and quick-witted. Definitely not the ninety-something year old I envisioned. I introduced myself and, in turn, he confided that although everyone used to call him Crazy Charlie they now just call him Charlie, at least when they thought he could hear them. But that was not his real name. He was Henry Charles Thomas III, but everyone laughed at him for having such a name and said he was crazy if he thought they believed he was a great grandson of a Scottish duke as he claimed.

I listened to him ramble on about his early days for some time. A fiction writer just never knows when they will run into a bit of information that will help develop a character. Besides the stories these old guys tell are extremely fascinating to me.

He had been raised in Iowa and came to central Montana in the mid-1940s after he got out of the Army. As a young infantry private during the D-Day invasion he was badly wounded and lost a leg. The Army patched him up and fitted him with a wooden leg then gave him a medical discharge and sent him home. He had been the only one in his entire platoon that survived the landing; maybe the only survivor of the whole company. He took a job herding sheep in central Montana so he could be alone and have time to work through his mental problems.

When he first came to Montana he just bummed around Lewistown for a while doing what few odd jobs he could find until he landed a job running sheep for George Meechum. George had a big spread up north on the other side of the Missouri River just south of the Belknap Indian Reservation. Charlie's range was in Coyote Coulee area up to Bull Creek. It was good sheep country except for the coyotes. The coulee came by its name honestly. Even the best herders had to keep a sharp eye out or they would lose a lot a sheep.

During that first year, Charlie admitted, he must have lost half his flock to those cagey coyotes. He just couldn't seem to be in the right place to chase away those varmits no matter how hard he tried. That fall he was sure old man Meechum was going to fire him for losing so many animals. He probably would have too, but several of the other herders reported large losses that season too. It seemed like the coyotes had been particularly active that year.

Charlie must have finally figured out the best ways to keep most of the coyotes away. He had tried a couple different sheep dogs, but they didn't help much to keep the coyotes away, although they did help by keeping him good company. Meechum considered him one of his best herders when they finally parted company several years later.

These first few years were tough ones for Charlie as he worked through his grief and relived the horrors of those few June days in Normandy when his world turned topsy-turvy several times over. The death and carnage all around him filled his memory, frequently spilling out with no warning to consume him at any time day or night. These episodes gave rise to his name Crazy Charlie.

Charlie fell silent with a distant, wishful look on his face. He didn't say anything as the minutes dragged by. I watched as Charlie seemed to transform, returning to those earlier days in the sheep camps he had come to love.

At last he spoke, his voice still sounding far away, "It was that dog that saved my life. I didn't know it then, but I learned the truth after he was gone."

I was afraid to respond to him. I didn't want to chance breaking through his train of thought and have the story disappear. But as his silence continued I decided I would try to get more from him. "What dog?" I asked.

"Seaman" was his simple reply.

I remained silent, sensing that he was ready to continue with his story.

He looked over at me with an apologetic smile, "Let me tell you the darnedest story I was ever a part of. Most people thought it was just more silly talk from old Crazy Charlie, but I swear to you this is all as true as night follows day."

With that Charlie launched into his story he said he could still remember as clearly as if it had all happened yesterday instead of fifty years ago.

He had been having a particularly bad day since early that morning when he found several dead sheep. He had been just a few minutes too late to prevent some coyotes from senselessly killing some of his sheep, apparently just for the joy of killing since there was no evidence of anything having fed on any of the dead carcasses. The freshly killed sheep were still warm.

This scene of wanton destruction had set him off. He watched as it turned into his re-occurring nightmare of his D-Day Normandy landing. The dead sheep became his platoon, all dead except him. Guns firing, shells exploding, men screaming in agony completed the chaos. In the midst of this terror he looked up the hill trying to find where the guns were in hopes he could figure out a way to stop them and their destruction. His leg was shattered, but he had to find a way to stop the guns or he would perish too. As he scanned the hill he spied a large black animal that he was sure was a wolf. Quietly raising his rifle he aimed and fired. The wolf quietly sat where he was. Charlie fired a second and a third shot, each one carefully aimed. The wolf calmly stood up and slowly trotted off over the crest of the hill.

Charlie interrupted his narrative, "I was an expert marksman in the Army and I had shot my share of coyotes and wolves while protecting my sheep, but this big black wolf just acted as if I was shooting blanks at him."

After the wolf disappeared over the hill, Charlie surveyed the scene of his dead sheep. He cleaned up the mess and buried everything so those damned coyotes would have no free food this time. When that chore was done he walked up the hill to where he had seen the wolf. He knew he had been re-living his nightmare of D-Day so he wasn't sure if what he had seen was real or not. Sure enough the tracks were there, visible in several places on patches of bare ground amidst clumps of grass and rock outcroppings. Mixed in with his tracks were several smaller coyote tracks.

Charlie's little sheep dog had disappeared sometime during the events of the morning. Charlie searched the area thoroughly for further tracks to try to determine where the coyotes had headed for. Not that it mattered much since he couldn't leave his sheep to follow the coyotes and hopefully get a shot at some. His search took him over the low, rolling hills backs to his camp where most of the sheep were calmly grazing. Charlie also found his dog fearfully hiding under the sheep wagon. When the dog saw Charlie he eagerly clambered out from under the wagon for a friendly greeting. He seemed to know all danger from those coyotes and that big black wolf were gone.

"That next morning just as it was starting to get light I heard the strangest howling that I had ever heard. I wasn't sure what it really was, but it didn't sound like a wolf or a coyote or anything else I know of. It was kind of a yapping like a coyote but not nearly high enough pitched. It was low like a wolf but wolves don't make any yapping sounds."

Charlie's voice trailed off so I could barely hear him then he continued, "It started almost like the bark of a dog; several high pitched barks then it seemed to transform to a long mournful howl ending in a kind of menacing growl."

"Are you absolutely positive that was the sound you heard?" I interrogated him.

"Just as sure as night follows day" came his reply. "I heard that same bark-howl every morning for the next week and always just as it was starting to get light. It always seemed to come from that hill where I saw that big black wolf."

Charlie continued with his story. After that first day he saw the black wolf he kept a sharper watch for coyotes. He saw that his sheep losses dropped to none. A few days later one morning while Charlie and his dog were making their tour of the sheep he saw the black wolf again. He was calmly sitting on a hillside watching Charlie and his sheep. The wolf made no effort to move when he heard Charlie's dog give a few tentative barks. The dog knew he was no match for that large, shaggy animal so he stayed real close to Charlie as he gave his barks that were a mixture of "hello" and "this is my territory." The wolf turned and gave the dog a look of acknowledgement then resumed his unflinching, far-away gaze.

That same scene was repeated for the next three days as dog and wolf seemingly came to terms. They weren't best buddies, but they weren't afraid or fighting each other.

"It was Sunday morning and the sun was well up in the sky when a dog barking interrupted my thoughts as I lay in the shade of my wagon," Charlie seemed to be thinking out loud.

"In fact it was so unexpected and so close it startled me. It was much deeper than my dog barked, besides he was asleep under the wagon. When I looked off to my left where the bark had come from that big black wolf was sitting on his haunches not fifty feet from me. It was crazy, but when he saw I had seen him he got up and trotted across the little valley about a quarter of a mile then set back down on his haunches as if he was waiting for me to follow him."

After another pause, "So I got up and followed him, walking leisurely until a got about a hundred feet away from him. Again he stood up and trotted away for about a quarter mile then set back down and waited for me to catch up. We repeated this a few more times until I realized he had taken me to the place I had found all those dead sheep a week earlier."

Charlie was quiet as if reliving the events he was telling me about, "One more time he stood and trotted up the hill I had first seen him on last week where he sat down to wait. This time I approached within a dozen feet of him before I stopped and sat on a large rock to wait for his next move. We remained in our spots for some time until he stood and walked a few steps to the edge of a small rock cliff face. I walked over to see what it was he had directed me to. Below us were the remains of at least eight coyotes, probably more. As I looked down in amazement the wolf turned and disappeared over the hilltop. I stood there a few minutes then I too departed, retracing my route to my camp."

The rest of the day was taken up by the weekly visit to Charlie's camp by Meechum's foreman bringing him a fresh supply of grub. They also discussed the status of the sheep and how the pasture was holding up. Fall was still some time off so the summer range would have to do for a while longer. The foreman left with his usual gruff admonition to keep a sharp lookout for coyotes so there would be some sheep left to drive down to the home place come fall. He did tell Charlie he was doing better and it looked like he hadn't lost very many sheep for the season.

When Charlie woke up the next morning the sun was already starting its arc across the sky. He was surprised he had slept so late. Then he realized there had been no wolf howling to wake him. A sudden fear gripped him as he hurriedly dressed and grabbed his rifle as he ran down the few steps from his wagon to the ground below. He had to see if his sheep were okay. If the wolf was gone had the coyotes returned?

To his relief all the sheep were scattered across the little valley in their little groups peacefully grazing. He could find no evidence of anything having been prowling around or any dead sheep. After satisfying himself that everything was as it should be Charlie returned to camp and prepared a late breakfast.

Since his sheep were all okay and he had found nothing that looked like coming trouble, he allowed himself the luxury to stay in camp and try to understand the events of the last week. A strange feeling of contentment pervaded Charlie. A feeling he hadn't had for years. He knew he had been witness to something very unusual. Something he would never completely understand.

As he pondered the events he had witnessed, he knew that big black wolf was definitely not a wolf. He had been within a few feet of the animal and recognized it as being some kind of a large black dog. He couldn't tell for sure because of its thick fur, but that dog must have weighed 150 pounds. It could run as effortlessly as the wind, disappearing from sight after only a few seconds. Charlie finally gave up trying to understand things he knew were beyond him. He had a large flock of sheep that needed his full attention and protection.

The days became shorter with the coming of fall and time to move the sheep down to the home ranch. With that done Charlie had no sheep to watch so he decided he would do some traveling. He knew some people down in Idaho Falls that he hadn't seen in years.

"I ended up spending all that winter in Idaho, mostly swapping stories with some other sheepherders I holed up with. One of the stories that I heard was an old Indian tale from the Nez Perces about a large black wolf/dog they could not kill. They shot it several times, but the arrows just went clear through that animal without doing it any harm. It was powerful medicine for them."

"That story made me think back on my experience earlier in the summer. I decided maybe I met that same wolf/dog because my bullets had just gone through it without doing it any harm."

Charlie looked over at me and mumbled in a low voice, "That wolf/dog was powerful medicine for me too. Old Crazy Charlie is tired now and needs to sleep."

He leaned back in his recliner and was soon softly snoring in peaceful sleep. I got up and quietly left. A glance at my watch showed 3:15 pm. We had talked for just over five hours without any breaks, not even for lunch. Charlie had earned his nap.

6 Charlie's Family

On my way out I stopped at the reception desk to see if Charlie had any family or friends that visited him. I was told that he had a grandson that came to see him once or twice a year and Charlie was quite fond of him. I got his name and address so I could contact him. I wanted to find out more about Charlie's mental state and maybe some more background. I figured that it would take quite a bit of digging to verify the most amazing story I had just heard.

I had my laptop with me, one of the few pieces of technology I carried with me when I went traveling. I sat down and sent off a quick introductory email to Charlie's grandson. That email quickly yielded much greater success than I could have possibly hoped for. Scott Thomas was scheduled to fly into Kalispell the next day from his home in Houston. He had a brief business meeting he had to tend to and he wanted to visit his grandfather. Beyond those two items he was free to meet with me. He was quite surprised that anyone would be interested in this aged sheepherder he called grandfather. He suggested a dinner meeting that evening after he arrived, if I would have time to wait around another day for him to arrive. So it was all set and I had a free day to go hiking up along the North Fork of the Flathead River. It should be a great time to think and shoot photos of the fall colors.

That evening when Scott walked over to my table I had to do a double-take. He was exactly how I pictured Crazy Charlie would have looked when he was much younger. Introductions made and Scott joined me. Our table was semi-separated from most of the other diners so we could talk without interruptions. I already liked Scott; he seemed to think of the necessary details.

Scott was surprised that anyone was interested in the stories his grandfather told of his long ago life. Surprised, but also pleased. Before he could inundate me with a slew of questions I gave him my brief account of why I came here to talk with his grandfather. I also told him the details of his story that I knew. I finished by stating that Charlie's story was hard to believe because I didn't have enough details for proof. I was generally sympathetic because I had heard the same bark-howl.

I went on to tell Scott that I wanted to get some idea of his grandfather's mental state. Was he aware of his environment, or was he living in the past, or his twisted version of it? How well could I believe what he said? And finally what could Scott add that would make his grandfather's story believable? What proof or even suggestions for further research did he have? Did he know anyone else who could validate Charlie's story? I assured Scott that I was not questioning his grandfather's sanity or credibility. It was simply that as a writer I had talked with many people over the years and learned the hard way to remain neutral on a new story until others are able to give some supporting evidence.

Scott told me without hesitation that his grandfather was totally sane. He gave no credibility that the nickname Crazy Charlie gave any indication of his mental state. His only problems were physical and probably normal for a 92 year old man.

At first Scott had been somewhat guarded toward me, but after he heard my story he was impressed because his grandfather had told me more than he had ever told anyone else, including Scott. He figured his grandfather must have taken a liking to me.

In reply to my question of what he knew about his grandfather's early life, Scott explained that he had spent a number of years putting together the pieces of a life of a man who had been a wanderer most of his adult life, so what he had was sketchy in places. He viewed his grandfather as a sincere, honest person that for some unknown reason just couldn't settle down to one place. He must have been friendly and a good worker because he had friends everywhere, and wherever he went he always had a job waiting for him.

Scott also told me that during his visits with his grandfather about half the time was spent talking about current happenings in the state and nation, what the family was doing, etc. He was very clear on everything. Charlie had taken a big interest in his great granddaughter who, at the age of ten, was developing into quite a basketball player. Scott said that his grandfather was looking forward to the day he could bring his whole family up to visit. Scott admitted that he had been hesitant about that , but by now had come to know his grandfather well enough that the family was planning a trip next year when school was out for the summer.

I asked Scott if there were more family members around that may have kept in touch with Charlie. Scott's smile was answer enough, but he said he was the only family member left since both his mother and father were gone. We weren't a very productive family until I came along. He proceeded to fill me in on Charlie's life.

When Charlie left Meechum's sheep outfit he landed in Idaho Falls as he had planned. He intended to spend a short while, maybe a couple weeks, visiting some friends, but it turned out that he spent the whole winter there. It seemed as though he met a gal by the name of Marion Foster and fell in love. That following summer he spent out west of Idaho Falls in the Three Buttes area tending a large flock of sheep. He must have managed to get at least some time off and got into Idaho Falls, though. That winter Charlie was back in Idaho Falls where he met his lady love and they got married. There was no work for him all winter, but he promised his new wife he would get a job come spring. Charlie had enough money for them to live on over the winter. He went to work for a farmer just out of town, but that only lasted until fall. Charlie was disappointed and very confused. Scott added, with a flicker of a smile, I don't think Charlie had quite figured out how to live with his new wife. She probably was a good part of his confusion. He ended up going back to Lewistown, Montana where he spent the winter. When he got back to Idaho Falls early that following spring he found that his wife was gone. He never did find out where she went.

Charlie started to wander and he never did settle down in one spot for very long until just a few years ago when he got to be so crippled up with age that he couldn't get around on his own. Scott said that his grandfather's wandering appeared to have started as he was looking for his wife. When he realized she was gone from him forever he never stayed in one place very long because he didn't want to chance finding and losing another love. He just lost interest in people, preferring the solitude of a sheepherder's life. He never knew that when his young wife left she was pregnant and later gave birth to a son she named William Thomas. He was Scott's father.

It's rather ironic but Marion never seemed to get over her separation from Charlie. She seemed to retreat from life to become quite reclusive, ending up in west Tennessee. Poor Marion only lived a few short years before she died. Her son was raised by relatives in St. Louis. It is odd how sometimes people do things that create a great tragedy in their lives, and maybe the lives of others too, because of not understanding something or some situation. Nobody ever knew why Marion left

Idaho without letting Charlie know where she was going.

Scott lamented that his grandmother's life was probably the biggest hole in his research on the Thomas family. Why she did what she did was a total mystery that nobody was at all willing to talk to him about when he had tried to find some answers.

"I never knew much about my dad" Scott told me, "He was quite young, maybe five or six, when he got dumped on his cousin's doorstep after his mother died. They raised him but never really accepted him into the family. He eventually quit school and joined the Army. He was sent to Vietnam where he was killed in combat. Some say he left for the Army just ahead of the very angry father of a pregnant daughter. Others say they had been married for several months before he left. They kept it from her family because they didn't approve of him"

Scott continued, "I was raised by my mother in St. Louis where I learned about the Lewis and Clark expedition because of my fascination with history. That same fascination with history is what has driven me to try and learn about my family. Genealogy is a great way to personalize history which makes it much more interesting to read. Grampa Charlie's story about Seaman has really piqued my curiosity."

He said that he had spent most of his time working on the Thomas family. My mother's family disowned us when they found out she had gotten married and was pregnant. He didn't even know if any of them still lived in the St. Louis area. He commented that he and his mother had to make it on their own the best they could.

He continued that he had been able to put together a very sketchy family tree for some of the Keslo family. It was primarily the ones that were in the St. Louis area. They were a big family that had scattered around the country. To make matters more complicated some of them wouldn't talk to other members of the extended family so brothers and sisters several generations back just disappeared.

Although this is quite normal according to genealogists, it requires considerable more time and travel to find the information and fill in the holes. Scott said he simply did not have enough time to spend on all the research he wanted to do.

He told me that the only other information he had found about his family was that his grandfather's folks left Iowa and returned to the ancestral homelands in Scotland. He had not been able to find any other of his family members living in the U.S. He had not done any research on his grandmother's family yet.

Scott wished me well on my research and asked if we could keep in touch. Because of his job he traveled quite a bit and didn't have much time to spend on research, but if he ran into anything he promised to pass it on to me.

7 NoDak

Charlie had mentioned that in his travels he had known some herders who had spent some time down on the Cannonball River in North Dakota. He thought one of them, a feller by the name of Hiram Olson, might be up around Bismarck if he was still alive. There was another guy in Williston by the name of Will Tanner. Charlie was sure that if they were still alive they would have some stories about Seaman for me.

He had told me these guys were a little older that he was. I was fearful that they might be too old to understand my questions. My calculations made him to be in his late eighties or early nineties. I was skeptical that I would have such good fortune twice, but I had to talk with them.

Like most of us who read history I just assumed that Lewis' dog had simply died a long time ago like people and dogs do. I was finding incidents of people having heard Seaman were much more common than I had ever imagined. The more time I spent talking to people and following leads, the more people I found who had information on my search, although most of it was bits and pieces from stories that people had heard long ago.

I got everything in order so I could take a quick trip over to North Dakota and talk to these guys. I had decided to take my pickup even though I would be traveling on highways and it would cost me more for gas that if I took my car. I had learned the hard way to always prepare for the worst. My car simply was not made for off road travel no matter how careful I tried to be with it. And when I got to talking with these people they insisted on showing me the areas they were talking about. The Missouri River breaks are not the best place to take any car.

My first stop was in Williston where I had found Will Tanner in the county nursing home. I had been warned by the staff there that Will had good days and bad ones. I brought a tape recorder with me just in case I hit one of the bad ones. I had also learned that when it came to talking with older people "good days" and "bad days" varied a lot in meaning. "Good days" to some may be "bad days" to others. When a person is fully coherent and I can stop them to repeat something or further explain during an interview, paper and pencil work best. But I had to be prepared for ramblings from a mind that was failing, so a tape recorder would be needed. At least I would capture everything he said so when I listened later I could replay anything I didn't quite hear or understand the first time.

I met Will at the nursing home and with the aid of an attendant we moved out to a patio in the warm

September sun. Will seemed in rare form, telling me about his days over on Six Mile Creek west of Marley. He homesteaded there were he raised a few pigs and chickens. The land wasn't much good but he was able to raise enough feed for the cows and sheep that he ran. He said it was a good place, but it was hard work to keep it producing.

I asked him if he remembered Crazy Charlie Thomas from his old days, maybe over in Idaho. His face lit up like a kid seeing a Christmas tree.

"My god yes. Is that old horse thief still alive and kicking" Will demanded?

"I just talked with him about a week ago" I replied. "He is living at the Old Soldiers Home in Columbia Falls, Montana."

"I know he is too blamed old to still be chasing sheep around the country. What's he up to these days? I haven't seen him since we was running sheep over in the Three Buttes. He was full of stories about his time on the Missouri River. Damdest story about a dog I ever heard."

I watched in dismay as the life seemed to drain from Will's face and he started to say something, but stopped after only a few words got out. He looked at me with a blank stare. Slowly life returned to him and he continued to talk. This pattern of fading in and out, then rambling talk continued for about an hour then Will fell silent. As I watched him he lowered his head until his chin rested on his chest. He was sound asleep.

I stopped my recorder and got an attendant who took Will back to his room. The attendant assured me that Will would sleep for several hours. They would probably need to wake him for dinner. Since he would not be eating lunch he would have to have dinner. I gathered my stuff and made my way back to my pickup hoping I could make some sense out of what I had on tape. The staff had been right and Will had held true to what they had told me to expect. He showed dementia, Alzheimer's, or whatever may be causing a failing mind was at times quite predictable.

I decided I needed to spend some time trying to sort out what Will Tanner had said while it was still fresh in my mind. Making sense of it all was sure to be like putting the pieces of a jigsaw puzzle together. I found my way to a city park on the bank of the Missouri River where I spread my notes and tape recorder on a picnic table. I spent several hours putting the pieces in order until I finally had the story I thought Will told me.

Will had been running sheep west of Idaho Falls when Crazy Charlie spent the winter there. They had met and passed the winter swapping stories. Will had told Charlie about the old Nez Perces legend of the wolf/dog that could not be killed. Indian arrows just passed harmlessly through him. He told Charlie about the bark-howl that was frequently heard around that part of the country. Although, Will admitted, he had never heard it himself.

Charlie told Will he had heard that same bark-howl over on the Missouri River in central Montana south of the Bear Paw Mountains. He talked to Will about a large wolf/dog that drove some coyotes away from his sheep.

I decided that I hadn't gained very much from this interview, other than someone saying the bark-howl had been heard in Idaho. But the Idaho Falls area was some distance from the trail the Lewis and Clark Expedition traveled. The other locations so far had all been on or very near their trail. I also saw that Will had not said anything about the bark-howl in the area of his homestead or anywhere around the Williston area.

I found the other sheepherder that Crazy Charlie had told me about. I met him at his house in Bismarck. I should probably be referring to him by his real name of Charles Thomas, but somehow Crazy Charlie fits him and just rolls off the tongue. Besides nobody that I had talked to when I was trying to find him knew Charlie Thomas and everyone knew Crazy Charlie.

Hiram Olson was fiercely proud of the fact that at just shy of one hundred years old—I later found out he was 98—he lived in his own house and took care of himself. He didn't need anyone to come check in on him or help him take care of any of his needs. He had outlived two wives, and several girlfriends; Hiram smiled and chuckled as he added the last part. It was hard to believe this guy was not in his early seventies.

He had spent many years working on his farm southwest of Shields down on the Cannonball River. It had been a good farm, but about a dozen years earlier he had decided to retire and had leased it out and bought a small house in Bismarck. Just in case something happened and he had to get to a doctor, as

Hiram said it. He still owned the house and outbuildings on the farm and sometimes he drove out for a visit. He had kept his Ford Ranger pickup when he left the farm.

Hiram continued with his blustery monologue about the farm and life and how in earlier times the Indians would cross the river from the Standing Rock Reservation to come visit him. They would always bring some fresh venison or antelope which would be traded for a bottle of Wild Turkey. With a smile he suggested he was simply carrying on the tradition of the explorers Lewis and Clark. After they left St. Louis on their way up the Missouri the first trade with the Indians was venison for whiskey.

"We would always get a good campfire going and roast the meat on a spit over the fire. While that was cooking we would crack open the Wild Turkey and spend the rest of the day in the enjoyment of good food, good drink, good people."

After a short lull while Hiram appeared to be reliving some time in his past, he looked at me and said, "We had to pay homage to the spirits of the Cannon Ball River."

"Yeah, a person's got to keep some traditions going" I mumbled under my breath.

Hiram gave me a frosty stare as he pushed a cup of freshly brewed coffee toward me. It was as if he thought I disapproved of his parties with the Indians. "I don't have any of the fluffy stuff they put in coffee these days. I probably could scare up some sugar if you want."

"Thanks, but no. I much prefer my coffee just like it is; none of that fluffy stuff to screw it up."

With a slight smile Hiram said, "Well at least we agree on that."

"Oh, we probably can agree on a lot more than that. I really don't care how much Wild Turkey you drink or who you drink it with. That's up to you. I sure don't criticize that any. Although in my day I liked Southern Comfort. But what I am really interested in is what Crazy Charlie told me you knew about the old Indian legends and Lewis' dog Seaman."

"Is Charlie still up to his usual ways? He sure was a story teller to beat all others when we were back in Idaho. But we all knew he wasn't exaggerating a bit when he talked about Seaman."

"Yeah, but he also warned me to keep a tight rein on you cause when you get to talking you could wander a long way off the subject. I suspect you weren't too far behind Charlie with our own stories."

"That's the same Crazy Charlie I knew" Hiram beamed broadly. "I haven't seen or heard from him for a long time. How's he doing?"

"He's at the Old Soldier's Home in Columbia Falls, Montana. I had a real good visit with him a short while ago. We talked for several hours and he told me about his days as a sheepherder in central Montana and southern Idaho. I also found out he had a son and a grandson. Until recently Charlie didn't know about either one."

"That's really good to hear. Charlie and I kept in contact for a long time, even though he was rambling all over the country. I finally lost track of him when he left Utah and headed for Nevada or Arizona, I never heard which. That's been 15 or 20 years ago. I guess I figured he must have cashed in by now."

"When he found out he had a son and a grandson and then the grandson started visiting him, Charlie really changed. The nurses say he looks and acts ten years younger."

"Poor Charlie; that woman sure threw him into a tailspin when she left that winter while he was gone. She never did get back in contact with him; didn't even tell him about his son. I always felt kind of sorry for him. She just didn't understand Charlie's situation. Those nightmares from the war really haunted him. Sometimes when he had an especially bad one he would just wander off and nobody would see him for days. I always wished there was something somebody could do for him."

"From what his grandson told me it must have been pretty hard on her too. She never remarried; in fact she became quite a recluse herself. I guess she just didn't know how to handle Charlie's nightmare problems."

"That's probably true. Poor guy, he just could not seem to get control of himself."

The silence lasted several minutes as we drank our coffee and reflected on our conversation; each of us deciding what to do from here. I thought Hiram was shutting me out and not really wanting to tell me what he knew about Seaman. I could only guess why, but I was sure he wasn't offended because of my comment about the Wild Turkey. But I could feel there was something making him hold his story inside. Then Hiram broke the silence.

"Yeah, I know all the legends. I have talked with Cheyenne and Nez Perces who had almost first hand experiences with the legendary black dog."

Another pause; it seemed as Hiram was trying to decide if he should open up to me or not. At length he must have figured I was okay. He continued.

"The Nez Perces tell the story of a large black wolf/dog that could not be killed. The arrows from the bravest warriors would simply pass through the animal without having any effect whatsoever. The people learned that when the black wolf/dog was in the area he had come not as an animal of prey to be hunted and destroyed, but to protect the children from other animals that were trying to harm them. The coyote, bear, mountain lion and wolf learned not to harm the children. They never knew when the black wolf/dog would see them. He would tell the people when he had come to see them by his unique bark-howl. When they heard him they knew the children were safe."

"It started up in northern Idaho when coyote had pushed a small child into the rapids on the Snake River. Suddenly a large black wolf/dog leapt into the river and pulled the small child from the water, setting him gently on the bank. He then caught coyote and told him that he was to never harm any of the children. He further instructed coyote to tell all the other animals about him and what happened and they were to never harm any of the children either. He, the black wolf/dog, would return from time to time to check on them."

Hiram continued, "The Sioux and Cheyenne both have stories about a large black wolf/dog that saved a boy from being trampled to death by a stampeding buffalo herd. A young man, hardly more than a child, was on his first buffalo hunt. As he closed to within a few feet of the buffalo he had selected to shoot he had his bow pulled back to launch the arrow when his horse stepped in a badger hole. Both horse and rider tumbled to the ground in the path of the stampeding herd. Suddenly a large black wolf/dog appeared and dragged the injured boy to safety behind a large rock. The herd split around the rock as it thundered across the prairie. When they had passed the boy was able to get help from the other hunters who carried him back home. That evening the black wolf/dog appeared near the boy's village and told the people he would protect the children from the dangers of the prairie animals. When they heard his bark-howl they would know he had come to see them."

"The Cannonball River is big medicine to the Sioux even today. That is why they were very insistent on it being part of their reservation. Even today nobody knows how all those perfectly round large rocks were made or appeared in the river."

"And that's why your afternoon feasting ceremonies with traded deer and Wild Turkey were important" I suggested.

I thought I detected some traces of an appreciative smile on Hiram's face as if he was saying, "You're getting the idea."

"The hill of the little devils is the other source for big medicine for these people. Many say that is where the black wolf/dog's powers came from.

I could see Hiram was getting very restless, and I thought that I detected he was very stressed or upset. But I was puzzled by his actions. It surely was nothing I had said since he was doing all the talking. Hiram couldn't sit still any longer.

He abruptly stood up with, "Excuse me a minute, I'll be right back." With that he almost ran out of the kitchen and down a short hallway to the rear bedroom. Before I had a chance to really decide what was happening he returned with several large three ring notebooks and a photo album. He walked over and handed them to me.

"Many years ago I started writing down my life experiences. The doctor suggested that it might help me come to grips with my nightmares. I haven't written anything for a long time so take these. They will help you understand."

Then in a gruff voice that was too loud for as close as he was to me, "I need to be alone now so just leave this old man with his memories."

8 Charlie's Funeral

When I got home from my trip to North Dakota I turned on my computer to go through my emails. I still don't like to be connected 24/7 as my kids say. I take my laptop with me but very seldom use it. I don't own any of the other new technology that everyone carries around with them. Sometimes my kids are sure I am the last of the surviving dinosaurs.

Most of my emails were spam and other stuff that disappeared with the touch of the delete key. But I did have a few I responded to. The last one almost got deleted, but luckily I reread the subject line. This one was from Scott Thomas telling me his grandfather had passed away and letting me know when the funeral would be. He hoped that I would be there. I wrote the date on my calendar to be sure and not miss it. From the tone of Scott's email he really wanted me there so he could talk with me.

I had several days before Charlie's funeral so I decided to start in on Hiram's notebook. I was more than just a little curious about it. But at the same time I was apprehensive, not wanting to get started only to have to put it aside before I was done. I know I sometimes get so totally lost in some of my projects I forget other important things. My wife assures me I will never die as long as I have my projects since I would forget my own funeral if she didn't remind me about it.

I finally decided to compromise and start by going through the album of photos Hiram had given me along with the three ring binder. So I spent the next few days examining the album, making notes about the photos I wanted to return to for a closer scrutiny at some later time.

Thanks to an early start I made the four-hour trip to Columbia Falls in plenty of time for Charlie's funeral services. The services were typically what a person would expect for an old man who had wandered the countryside most of his life without ever putting downs roots anywhere. He undoubtedly had hundreds of acquaintances across the country, but very few friends. Consequently there were only a handful of people to witness a quick service that was followed by a VFW firing party who saluted a fallen comrade in arms.

Scott was the only family that came to Charlie's funeral so after the services we went to a local coffee shop where we could talk. He told me he had a couple things on his mind to discuss with me.

He said that during the few weeks after his grandfather had talked to me about Seaman he seemed to change. Charlie always had a nervous energy about him; he just couldn't settle down even though he was barely able to walk on his own; he appeared constantly fearful about someone or something.

Scott told me the best that he could figure out was that Charlie was able to focus on his life as he recounted his experiences to me. He somehow must have let the "powerful medicine of that wolf/dog" work on him and chase away all of the D-Day nightmares. Charlie had told him they were gone and he was at peace now and ready to settle down and accept life as it was. He knew he would soon be gone.

"Charlie wanted me to pass his thanks on to you for taking an interest in his story and listening to him ramble on for hours. He knew you understood because you knew the bark-howl."

I told Scott that after I had talked with Charlie that day I sensed that he changed. All day he had been restless and fidgety. As the day wore on he didn't tire as the nurses had told me he always did, but seemed alert as if he wanted, or needed, to get his story out. When he finished he became very calm and easily drifted off to sleep as the "medicine" took effect.

We drank our coffees in silence for several minutes, just letting Charlie slip peacefully away. At length Scott brought us back to reality. He told me he had found that he had a cousin still living in St. Louis who had known his father, William Thomas. They had talked about the family connection he had found through his genealogy research. He had also told her about my research on Seaman and the bark-howl. She said that if I ever made it to St. Louis with my research to be sure to look her up.

Scott had a plane to catch to get back to Houston and I needed to get home to start examining Hiram's notebook. We somewhat reluctantly said our goodbyes and went our separate ways with promises to stay in touch.

On my drive home I decided that before I plunged into Hiram's notebook I would review what Lewis and Clark had written in their journals about the Spirit Mound and the Cannonball River. They both appeared to be important to Hiram; he referred to them as being considered big medicine by the tribes that had lived in the area. I was not very familiar with either and didn't want to chance overlooking something Hiram wrote, like I almost did with his story about feasting with the Indians out at his farm.

Clark first mentions a river the French called "La Boulet" where he saw a great number of perfectly round stones in the bluff and on the shore that resembled cannonballs. He wrote that the river takes its name from these stones.

During the winter of 1804-1805 the Expedition spent at Fort Mandan Lewis prepared a volume of their first year's travel intending to send it to President Jefferson. One list he made was titled "Mineralogical Collection" which had descriptions of many things he had observed along with descriptions of specimen he was also sending to the President. Lewis wrote, "incrustations of large round masses of rock which appear in a sand bluff just above the entrance of the Cannonball River. Many of them are as perfectly globular as art could form them." Lewis must not have been the first to let his imagination run a little bit wild to imagine some mysterious force or person that formed these rocks and decorated the river's edge with them. The Indians of times past must have seen something unusual for them to call this big medicine.

The Expedition journal keepers didn't record anything about ceremonies being held in this area or speak of scared locations, but they never talked to any of the natives about this area of the river.

Clark describes "Spirit Mound" as a conical shaped high hill set in an immense plain. Clark continues by telling the Indian story of Spirit Mound. It was the home of devils in human form 18 inches tall and very watchful with sharp arrows to kill at great distances anyone who attempts to approach the hill. Their belief of this was so strong that nothing could induce any of the tribes to approach the hill. The Captains decided to visit the "mountain of evil spirits" the following day.

After they return Clark gives a full description of the strange hill. "The base of the mound is a regular parallelogram the long side of which is about 300 yards in length the shorter is 60 or 70 yards. The base rises with steep ascent to a height of 65-70 feet leaving a level plain on top 12 feet wide and 90 feet long. The north and south part of this mound is joined by two regular rises each in oval form. The regular form of this hill would justify a belief that it owed its origin to the hand of man."

He concluded his remarks, "after examining this mound it is my opinion that sufficient proof to produce a confident belief of all the properties of which they ascribe it."

During the Captains trip to the Spirit Mound Seaman got so overheated and fatigued they had to send him back to camp to cool off and rest. Lewis and several of the other men who were along also experienced much fatigue, becoming very hot, and great thirst. Lewis wrote on August 24, 1804 one of his very rare journal entries during this part of the expedition. He said, "This day the chronometer (watch) stopped just after being wound up; I know not the cause but fear it proceeds from some defect which is not in my power to fix."

This discussion about Spirit Mound was 23-24 August of 1804. There wasn't anything else written about Seaman until eight months later when Lewis noted on 29 April 1805 that Seaman caught antelope while swimming in the river, the same way that the wolves did.

9 Hiram's Notebooks

After taking care of a few matters that demanded my attention when I got home, I was finally ready to start examining in detail the notebooks Hiram gave me. I had already gone through his photo album. It had been filled with the normal photos of men working and ranch life.

There were a few photos I had marked with notes to use when I examined them in detail later. These included some sheep killed by coyotes, a Newfoundland dog and Hiram with his two sheep dogs. Another one was of Crazy Charlie and his wife.

Hiram's photo album would normally have been the perfect complement to a book on early day sheep ranching. They were a good combination of people working and playing. His photos captured animals and activities common to the ranches. There were also some good landscape photos that exhibited the vast open spaces and solitude sheep herders lived in. I was hoping for more in his writing since Hiram had suggested by his abrupt actions it was anything but normal life he had captured.

With coffee in hand I started reading the first notebook. Although it was handwritten Hiram had good penmanship so his writing was quite easy to read. I soon found out he was also a good writer. The more I read the more I became convinced he had formal training and considerable experience as a writer.

I had been reading for several hours when I came to a page that had a few lines on it, then some ink blotches, words crossed out, and in general just a mess. This was followed by a few more lines with more stuff crossed out, then lines of just words. Everything was confused and the words didn't seem to fit together. They were more like a bunch of words randomly written. This continued for two pages and finally ended towards the bottom of a third page. It looked as if Hiram was really struggling with himself; if he could just keep putting words on the page he could overcome some monster that was trying to take control of him.

These pages were quite a shock to me. What I had read for the last two hours appeared to be a good start on a book of Hiram's memoirs. I had begun to think he had been writing the text to go with his photos I had looked at earlier.

It was getting dark so I reluctantly put Hiram's notebook aside to tend to my daily chores. I would return to it later.

After supper I picked up Hiram's notebook to continue my reading. When I turned the page at the end of his pages of confused words all I saw was lines and scribbling much like a two or three year old child might do. Another page of similar scribbling followed except the word "dog" was neatly printed at the very bottom of that page.

I was almost afraid to turn the next page. I didn't know what to expect. I looked away as I flipped the page. As my gaze wandered back to the notebook I couldn't hold back a smile of relief when I saw a page full of Hiram's neat writing. The stories of his sheep days continued as if there had been no interruption.

I spent the rest of the evening reading Hiram's memoirs. He was not writing a chronological biography, but simply telling stories about his life. I saw some from his early childhood and some about time in the army. However most were while he was a sheepherder in Idaho and several other states as he wandered about plying his lonely trade caring for his sheep.

I still had a lot of reading ahead of me, but it was easy reading. Hiram had a way of writing that captured the reader's full interest and made him feel as if he was sitting beside a campfire somewhere listening to Hiram talk. I had a mental picture of a scene with several people around Hiram leaning in close so as not to miss a word of what was said.

Hiram's notebooks consumed my time for a week as I read and reread what he had written. I found a pattern to his work. As he labored to overcome his innermost problems he had produced a very fine quality book length memoir complete with photos that greatly enhanced the work. Scattered throughout his writing were sections of scratched out words, ink blobs, random words, and just plain scribbling. At the bottom of the last page of each of these series of jumbled pages was neatly printed "dog."

These notebooks painted a picture of a man who had been born into abject poverty, but found a way to get away from of a life he rejected. He was well educated, but had "itchy feet" and for many years simply could never settle down. He was too interested in seeing the world around him.

When World War II drew the United States in, Hiram did what he thought was his duty and enlisted in the Army. He spent three years fighting in the European Theatre. Although he came through all the battles without injury, he returned to the United States a mental wreck. His experiences of seeing extensive death and destruction, so typical of war, left him almost totally incapable of functioning in a normal peacetime society. He had escaped from a prisoner of war camp and evaded capture several other times. Those experiences left him very fearful of people.

He could not survive in society so was forced into a solitary life on the prairies or mountain foothills tending his sheep. His sheep and dogs were the only ones he could trust.

With the passing of time Hiram learned to hide his mental wounds by adopting a facade of bravado showing how tough he was. Because he was a good sized man and in visibly good shape he was able to defuse most confrontations by threats that caused the other man to back down.

Over a period of years Hiram eventually learned to cope with himself and society well enough that he gave up the solitary life of sheepherding. He went to southwest North Dakota where he purchased a modest sized farm. He still had his rough times, but he worked hard at fitting into society, even getting married. But his marriages, or even long term relationships, never lasted. He finally gave up on that kind of companionship and contented himself with being a bachelor; he used tell his acquaintances that he was too old to break in a new partner.

He had spent almost thirty years working his farm on the Cannonball River. His stories showed me they were years of hard work, but farming always has been everywhere. Hiram was proud of his farm. It had given him a good life and provided him with a good income.

One of the stories during this part of his life was about a feast with some of the Sioux from the reservation that was across the river from his farm. This must have been the tradition he had been referring to when we had been talking at his home in Bismarck.

This story struck me as being different. The others were well organized and well written. This story was in pieces, somewhat incoherent and quite repetitive. At first I thought he wrote it while he was under the influence of some of that Wild Turkey whiskey he had told me about. Then I wondered if he wasn't writing in that style to create an effect of how the feast actually turned out. But neither reason passed close scrutiny. I reread this story several times trying to figure out why it was different from everything else he had written.

I set Hiram's notebooks aside for a few days while I took care of a few matters that needed my attention. This time was ideal to mull over in my mind what I had just read.

When I returned to my project I realized that if I took out the pages of scribbles, Hiram's memoirs were nearly ready to publish; just add photos from the album and it was ready to edit. But what were the scribbles all about? Why the word "dog" at the end of each set? Who was the big black dog in the photo album? All the other photos had captions telling what they were about.

I marked each section of scribbling then carefully removed each one so I could concentrate on them. I had already examined the complete notebooks and could find nothing in the memoir text that could have triggered Hiram to write the scribblings. I wanted to see if they were similar in any way other than "dog" at the end.

I spread them out on a big table and started my examination. Each of the episodes lasted for five pages and followed the same pattern of lines crossed out, ink blotches, random words, scribbly lines and "dog" at the end.

As I examined these entries I noticed they all started by repeating the last few lines of what had been written just above. It looked like maybe Hiram realized that and scratched them out. That was his last coherent act before a bitter fight with the devils for control of his mind started in earnest. He kept writing as a way to fight them off, but eventually they won and the words became nothing but scribbling lines. Then something would happen and Hiram would re-gain control and the episode would end.

I wondered if Hiram was fighting the same nightmare in every episode. What was it that set him off? Could I find any answers in the random words he wrote? What really struck me was why Hiram wrote when these episodes hit him. What made him decide to write his memoirs?

After what I considered to be a thorough examination of the words Hiram wrote during these episodes I was still at a loss. Some of the words overlapped from one episode to others, but I could find no consistent pattern. Common words were war and war related, words referring to nature, and his being trapped, but they were not all used in all episodes. I finally decided he just put down any word that came to his mind. Maybe the particular words weren't what were important. Maybe the act of writing was what was important.

I had to set Hiram's notebooks aside for a while so I could work through in my mind what I had been reading. I understood and enjoyed most of what I read of his memoirs. In fact, I had made a mental note to talk with my publisher about getting his book into print. I figured it wouldn't be very much more work to get them ready. He had obviously worked on them, even to the extent of getting captions for the photos.

But first I had to come to terms with the sections of his scribblings. I had to figure out what to do with the stories that stopped in mid-sentence or were otherwise left muddled and incomplete. Hiram had returned to a few of them and tried to fix them, but he was not successful in his efforts. They still looked patched up and somewhat amateurish, like a child had written them. I was not sure if I could give them an acceptable finish, or even if I wanted to try.

My mind was going in circles. Hiram had insisted I take his notebooks to answer my questions about Seaman. He said if I read them I would understand. However, except for a few pages of scribbling, everything seemed to be a very well done memoir of a working man's life as he rose from poverty to a landowner and well-respected member of the community he lived in. While they did show a life of a man who overcame the nightmares of fighting in a war, I could not find any clues to solving my puzzle of why people said the bark-howl was Seaman.

10 War is Hell

I received a letter from Hiram telling me that I should keep the notebooks and photo albums and do with them as I wish since he had no family to pass it on to. He said that he had always thought that one day he would try to get his memoirs published, but he no longer had the energy needed to do the job. He had decided that what had started out just as a very personal struggle to overcome his mental terrors had become a passionate adventure. The writing and the photography captivated him to the point he sometimes spent more time on them than he did on the farm.

He wrote, "I've lived long, worked hard and enjoyed my life of freedom. I started with nothing but a strong determination to make a better life for myself than the one my father had. He died young working for an uncaring tyrant who was only interested in the profits his business produced for him. My father left a wife and several children who all perished at early ages still in abject poverty except me.

You know Seaman and have seen his power; you have heard his bark-howl. He healed me. He healed Charlie. How or why he selected me I will never know, but without him I would never have survived my ordeal with the terrors of war. In my times of need when I was scribbling my worst I heard his bark-howl and knew I would be okay. He protected us just like he protected the Cheyenne, Sioux and Nez Perces. I guess we were his children too. All of the Indian legends grow from Seaman's return to the prairies after Captain Lewis died. Spirit Mound was calling him.

I am on old man now and the doctor tells me I can't live much longer. Since I have no family remaining it would please me greatly if you would consent to take care of my matters when I am gone. There's not much beyond my little farm and my house here in Bismarck. Neither one is of great financial value; do with my estate as you think proper. My only other request is that after all expenses are paid, give any remaining cash to the North Dakota Historical Society."

Hiram's letter only added to the confusion in my mind. How did he think I knew Seaman? I had only heard a very unusual howling that early morning on the cliffs above the Missouri River. I surely didn't know anything about his power and I did not understand what Hiram or Charlie had been healed of.

I had learned everything I could from Hiram's notebooks so I set them aside. I took the liberty of at least temporarily keeping the sections of scribbling separate from the rest of the memoirs. I suspected he was suffering from World War II nightmares like Crazy Charlie had been. I couldn't be sure since I didn't know enough about his war experiences. My next step was to learn more about his mental condition.

I saw absolutely no connection between a dog that lived two hundred years ago and a new exotic mental disease. I had heard someone say all soldiers who go to war suffer post traumatic stress syndrome (PTSD). However I had passed that off as someone who was trying to make a name for himself with some new breakthrough medical research. I had seen any number of people who had returned from combat and were as normal as anyone else.

I was skeptical about what I could do, but I figured that I owed Hiram at least a little bit of research. I turned to my computer and started my quest to find more information about Hiram's mental problems. From the several thousand websites my google search provided I went to the Veterans Administration website to see what they had to say. After reading that site I carefully read through several other sites belonging to public health agencies, psychologists and mental health physicians. I became quite engrossed in what I was finding. This whole subject that I thought was something new actually goes way back in time; some say as far as the Roman Legions in the days before Christ.

The modern study of PTSD, I found, breaks down into three periods; WW II, Vietnam, and Iraq. Although named for wars, experts now say PTSD is not limited to a war situation, but can result from almost any physical ordeal that has some traumatic results associated with it. Almost everyone exhibits some of the symptoms of PTSD following an ordeal, but most people overcome these effects after a short while. This is what is called the normal grieving process. However, to the extreme, a few people can never overcome the effects. As a result these are the ones that commit suicide.

We first knew PTSD during WW II and earlier as battle fatigue or shell shock or exhaustion. The treatment was to send the soldier to an area where they weren't doing any fighting for a short rest break. This could be a short stay in a hospital if the soldier was wounded. Many times it turned out the wounds were self-inflicted as a part of the withdrawl or escape symptoms or to overcome the guilt of having been spared by the battle while the others died. Not much was understood about this disorder. It was a period when men were supposed to be tough and not let problems in your head get you down. Be a man and don't fear anyone or anything. This was particularly true for soldiers in time of war.

An excellent example of this period was when General Patton was visiting wounded soldiers in a field hospital and giving out medals to the men for their combat deeds. He saw a young private who was crying. After a sharp exchange of words the General slapped the Private and ordered him back to his unit. This incident soon became known to the commanding general of the European Theatre, Dwight Eisenhower, who made Patton publicly apologize to the Private.

This incident was kind of the beginning of the end of Patton's military career.

Other evidence of PTSD during the early period was the hobos, or bums, who aimlessly wandered the country escaping from their fears. They were loners who frequently were either into fights or hopelessly drunk. People would simply disappear and never be heard of again.

The next period which was called the Vietnam period is probably best known for the widespread use of illegal drugs by military personnel and veterans as a means of escaping the ravages of their mind and what they saw during the war. The drugs would numb their minds so they would not have to deal with their problems.

The modern period, which is sometimes called the Iraq period, is often credited with a more thorough understanding of the nature of this mental disorder. Mental health professionals have recognized more symptoms and now realize the disorder is caused by more than just war. It can be many different encounters that produce extreme physical or mental strains. It is now recognized that car wrecks, criminal actions and natural disasters can cause PTSD as much as war can.

As I read more from the websites I had selected I began to compare both Crazy Charlie and Hiram to the symptoms of PTSD. They had shown lack of involvement or dropping out of the main stream of society and turned to the loner life of a sheepherder. Neither of them could maintain a long-term personal relationship and they both suffered through their recurring bouts of nightmares. Both men admitted guilt because they survived when so many others had been killed. It was becoming quite clear to me they suffered PTSD, undoubtedly resulting from their WW II war years.

Hiram's notebooks were beginning to make more sense to me now. One of the theories I had read about was called "exposure theory" and said that the best way to overcome the problems is to face them head on. The natural instinct is to avoid a place or situation that traumatizes a person. It's like avoiding an intersection where you previously had a car wreck. Elements of the theory include visiting the place of the event and talking about the event with others. Writing about it is a good substitute for talking about the event.

It was time for me to stop reading and just think for a while. There were literally hundreds of pages of material I had read. After a while it all started flowing together to the point I wasn't sure if it was getting very repetitive or if my mind was getting overloaded and making it that way. I definitely didn't want to get so overloaded that I missed some detail that might go a long way in explaining my search. I had to see how much I understood about what had been happening. I reached over and closed out my computer browser, then after stacking the pages of my notes into a file folder, I leaned back in my chair and closed my eyes.

This whole thing about Seaman reminded me of those detective shows on television. They get a lot of bits and pieces of information then spend great amounts of time and energy trying to figure out how the pieces fit together. When they eventually make things fit they are able to solve the crime.

I wasn't trying to solve a crime, but I had accumulated quite a few bits and pieces to a puzzle I was faced with. Why were these few people so convinced that what they, and what I too had heard, was Captain Meriwether Lewis' dog Seaman? How could that even be possible? Seaman had lived two hundred years ago. How could a dog's bark be so unique that it defied identification as to whether it was coming from a dog, wolf, coyote or some other animal?

It was time to see just what details I had put together and see if I could start answering some of my questions, or at least see if they pointed me in some direction for more investigating. A thorough review would allow me to organize my notes so I could make some sense out of what I had learned.

The telephone broke through my thoughts as it rang; I'm not sure how many times. Whoever was on the other end of the line was either extremely patient or very determined. When I finally realized the noise that interrupted my thoughts was the phone I answered it.

Scott Thomas was calling to see if I was interested in a trip to St. Louis. After many years of living scattered across the country and never seeing each other, Charlie's family was planning to hold a union/reunion. Since Charlie had died they discovered each other. There was hardly more than just a handful of close family members, but they wanted to meet each other. They might find out there were more of them than they realized. St. Louis seemed to be a good central location.

They had been having problems getting a date for their reunion that was good for everybody. Finally someone took the initiative and said here is the date and place; make it if you can. That date was about ten days off. Scott was somewhat apologetic for the short notice, but he had just realized that I might be able to find out more of my puzzle at the reunion.

I checked my calendar and found that I had nothing scheduled that could not be re-scheduled so I told Scott I would be there.

For some reason Hiram had tied his life and Charlie's life together beyond just spending some of their early days together tending sheep. I got to thinking that if I learned more about Charlie's family maybe it would help unravel the mystery of both men. A family reunion could be interesting.

11 Reunion

I got to St. Louis the afternoon before the Thomas/Keslo family get together was scheduled. Since I was not at all familiar with the city I wanted to look around a little and kind of get my bearings. The reunion was going to take place outside in the park since the weather was still warm. I found an adequate room in a small motel close to the park so I could easily walk to the reunion and avoid all the traffic.

There was a nice café across the street from my motel. The coffee wasn't Starbuck's, but it was satisfactory. The waitress told me it was roasted locally by a small company that only sold their coffees to a few selected retailers. I felt good to patronize local business instead of the big box stores.

I'm not much on fancy foods, but the waitress insisted I try their "world famous barbecue ribs." She said the recipe they used had been in the family for several generations. Over the years it had won many awards at county fairs throughout the region. She wouldn't tell me what all went into the barbecue sauce, but having been developed in the south, Kentucky primarily, some of the liquid was undoubtedly bourbon. I couldn't resist her sales pitch, I really didn't try too hard, so I gave in and ordered some.

I didn't need to eat very much before I fully understood why they were so well known and liked. Foods do not normally impress me, but these barbecue ribs sure did. Although I am not a big eater, I consumed more than my share of those ribs. I knew I would suffer later, but once in a while it is worth the suffering.

As I was finishing off the last few bites of this most delicious meal I heard a familiar voice, "Looks like you started the reunion without the rest of us."

The voice was Scott Thomas who had just come into the little restaurant. He had with him a woman and several kids ranging in age I estimated from six to fifteen. Scott introduced them as his wife, Karla, then rattled off the names of four kids. I must admit the only one I remembered was the youngest. Being the only boy, he carried the family heritage with a name of Henry Charles Thomas IV, but he went by Charlie, as he proudly announced to me. A picture formed in my mind of Crazy Charlie as a beamingly proud great grandfather who was obviously more than happy to share that name.

"I'm not sure who I have reunioned with other than a very delicious meal of barbecue ribs, along with some tolerably good locally roasted coffee."

"You have managed to find the official Thomas/Keslo family reunion headquarters. This place is owned and operated by a cousin of mine, Kathy Keslo. Her brother, Roger, is the coffee roaster you referred to. Their grandmother, Laurie Keslo, raised my father after his mother, my grandmother, died."

"I didn't know I had fallen into the main nest. I thought I had just found a friendly little place that served great food. The young lady that waited on me didn't say who she was or even that she owned the place."

"That's the way Kathy is. She lets her food do the talking for her."

While Scott and I had been talking his wife disappeared. When she returned she had Kathy Keslo with her. She made the introductions.

"If your food talks for you as Scott tells me, it is screaming great things about you now" I chided Kathy.

"Has he been giving out all my secrets again?" Kathy smiled as she played along.

"Just a few of the least important ones. Being the honorable gentleman he is he wouldn't think of divulging a lady's best kept ones."

"What a line of bull" Scott cut in, "it's really getting deep in here."

The spell was broken. We pulled several small tables together with mine to make room for Scott and his family. Kathy disappeared to return shortly with plates of food. It looked to me like she had brought enough to feed the proverbial army, but by the time we finally left, every plate was clean. Four growing kids had bottomless pits for stomachs and any food in sight seemed to just disappear.

During the meal Scott and Karla gave me a brief rundown of the Keslo family tree and those that they understood were planning to be at the reunion the next day. Nobody had very big families; most were only one or two kids; a few never married. And, like so many extended families, some of the clan refused to have anything to do with the rest of the group.

They started with the matriarch of the family, Laurie Keslo. She had married and had one son, Earl. Her husband, Scott couldn't remember his name, had died during the Korean War.

Earl had married and they had two kids. A daughter Emily, who lived in California, had never married. The other was a son, Arthur, who was Kathy and Roger's father.

Earl was a fighter pilot during Vietnam and developed a strong liking for "wine, women, and song." His wife, Marie, eventually divorced him amid some very colorful stories about Earl. She brought the two kids back to St. Louis to live.

Earl had been an only child until Scott's father William, was dumped on his family's doorstep to raise when his mother died. Earl always resented William for making him share his mother and father's attentions.

Arthur had died at an early age from cancer. His widow remarried an Air Force officer and left St. Louis for a life traveling the world with her new husband. They kept in contact, but everyone seemed to be busy with their own lives.

Laurie had two older brothers. They had left home at an early age to seek their fortunes elsewhere.

Neither one wanted to live in the city. They just wanted to be farmers. They did not stay in contact with the rest of the family so nobody knew much about them or any family they might have.

Scott added the Thomas family was to his knowledge all gone here in the United States. He had heard that when his great grandfather and great grandmother (Crazy Charlie's parents) in Iowa died Charlie's two sisters returned to Scotland and wanted nothing to do with the United States or anybody living in that terrible country that had killed their parents. There still were some of the family living in Scotland, but all of the attempts he made several years ago to establish a contact with them were rebuffed.

They told me that was about it for the family. Not very many left living close by. There were others scattered around the country, but neither Scott nor Karla knew the names or what the kinships were exactly. They had heard that others were coming to the reunion and were eager to see who showed up and what kinds of stories would be told.

We had all managed to stuff ourselves well beyond what we knew we should have with Kathy's outstanding food, so everyone left to rest up and prepare for the coming day. It could prove to be quite interesting or, more than likely, turn out to be just a pleasant day of casually meeting new people.

In the solitude of my motel room I pondered the family backgrounds Scott had told us about, wondering what there was that he thought I would find relevant to my search for Seaman. Why had he asked me to come to the reunion? I found no clues to that, but I decided to leave my options open and be ready to quickly record things just in case. I packed my camera in its bag along with extra batteries and a few other essentials, then added a pen and notebook just to be sure.

As I drifted off to sleep I thought about how I would work it to have brief conversations with as many people as possible at the reunion to determine if they had any information that could in any way contribute to my quest. I would need to interview each one, but I wanted to make it appear to be just friendly, casual conversation. If something of interest came up that might take some time I would make arrangements for a follow up meeting later. I decided the easiest way would be for me to assume the role of an acquaintance of Crazy Charlie. I had met him through the grandfather of an old classmate of mine that I got reacquainted with many years after we graduated from high school. Since this was basically true it would not be too difficult for me to play the role and make it believable.

After a breakfast of coffee and toast—I was still full from the barbecue ribs I ate the night before—I decided to wander over to the park area where the Keslo/Thomas family was going to hold their reunion. There were a few other people in small groups scattered here and there, but I had no idea if any of them were early arrivals for the reunion or just other folk enjoying the great outdoors. I sat down at an empty table with thoughts of checking my email then getting a few photos of the area.

Just as I finished and closed up my laptop I noticed a small group of people nearby that seemed like they wanted to say something to me but were uncertain if they should. With my friendliest voice and a smile bigger than a used car salesman I gave my best good morning.

That was all it took to break the ice. With the conversation that ensued I found out they were indeed part of the Keslo clan. They had never had any contact with the rest of the extended family, but they had heard about the reunion and decided it was a good chance to meet some relatives. They were from southern Idaho, around the Idaho Falls area.

They weren't sure if they were in the right place but had been afraid to ask anyone. None of them had ever been to a city the size of St. Louis and didn't know if the stories they had heard were true or not about strangers in big cities. I told them they had made a good choice since I too was a visitor to the city. I said that I was from a little town of Great Falls, Montana. Of course they knew where Great Falls was and we were soon talking like long lost friends.

I found out the group I was talking with, or listening to as they talked, was Ray and Simon Paul and their families. They had farms northwest of Idaho Falls, in the same area where their grandfather Silas Paul had first farmed. Later his only son, Ernest Paul, took over the farm. Ernest was Ray and Simon's father, but was not in god enough health to make a trip to St. Louis for the reunion.

Ray continued to give me a brief rundown on his family connection to the reunion. His grandfather Silas was Laurie Keslo's older brother. He had started his farming life working as a sheepherder for a short time around Idaho Falls before he saved enough money to buy some farm land. He had heard of Crazy Charlie and his stories and had met him.

Silas and Laurie's other brother, Wilbur, had also spent his life farming, but he had gone farther north to eastern Washington. When he got too old to run the farm he sold it and moved to Spokane since none of the family wanted to farm. His small family scattered across Washington and Oregon pursuing their life dreams. A few went as far south as Arizona, but Ray and Simon didn't know what they were doing or exactly where in Arizona they were living.

For some reason that part of the family had never made any attempt to make contact with the rest of their relatives. Ray mentioned that rumors came up periodically that several of them were trying real hard to keep a few steps ahead of the law so they were never eager to say exactly where they were living.

I saw by my watch it was getting late into the morning so I suggested that we might walk over to Kathy's café to see if any of the rest of the family was there. Scott had referred to the café as the reunion headquarters. I didn't know if he was serious or not, but we hadn't met any more of the reunioners. It was worth a try.

Sure enough when we walked in the door the café was filling up. I recognized Scott and his wife so I assumed the others were more of the family. I took the little group over to where Scott was and introduced them. Scott confirmed that everyone in the place was part of the extended family reunion. He was doubly pleased by the morning's events. First there was a much larger turnout than he had expected. Second when he found out that some of his grandmother's brothers' family came to the reunion. He had never met any of them before. He wasn't even sure if any of that part of the family knew about the reunion, but hoped that somehow they had heard and at least a few would come.

While we talked several more groups squeezed their way into the small café. Kathy managed to work her way over to where Scott was. After a brief exchange they agreed it was time to move the group outside to the park where there was room to spread out and be comfortable. Besides with everyone talking the noise level in the café was so high the only way to be heard was to almost scream into the ear of whoever you were talking to. We moved a short distance over to a section of the park that had been set up with many picnic tables so everyone could sit down instead of trying to balance food and drinks then try to eat and talk.

I decided food could wait, and with fresh hot coffee in hand I wandered from one group to another as I tried to meet as many as I could. As I moved about saying a few words or just listening to some of the casual conversations I realized there wasn't going to be a lot of information gathered here. However, I still held out hope for a few leads. These were just down-to-earth, everyday folk gathered to meet relatives they had heard about, but never seen before. The numbers had grown from the small handful Scott had anticipated to well over a hundred. Somehow the word had spread and relatives decided to attend. It probably would be one of those extended family events that would only happen once, but it would be remembered within the family and talked about for years to come.

My coffee was empty so I decided I would find a place to get a refill. With a full cup of coffee in one hand and a delicious looking cherry cobbler in the other I was looking for a place to sit when a voice beside me called my name. I looked around and saw Ray who motioned me over to join them.

"Looks like you need a place to sit. You are welcome to join us. We have room here for you."

"Thanks. I'm not really very good at balancing all these and eating them too."

"Hey that cobbler looks good. Almost as good as the last two pieces I had" Simon chimed in. "Guess I better try just a little bit more" as he ambled over to the tables full of desserts.

"He acts as if he never gets fed at home" Ray confided in me "but his wife's a great cook and he eats that way all the time. I just don't understand why he never gains any weight."

"Yeah, I just gained five pounds looking at this" I chuckled as I forked a bite into my mouth.

I asked Ray if they were meeting a lot of the relatives they never really knew they had. He told me that everyone seemed talkative and friendly, but once the hellos were all said then the relationships figured out there wasn't much more said. Being farmers in a very rural area of the country they didn't have much in common with the city folk. The only things left to talk about were religion and politics, but they were taboo since nobody wanted to risk starting a big fight.

Both Ray and Simon were hoping to meet their great aunt Laurie, but since she was the matriarch of the extended family everyone else wanted to meet her too. Both their grandfather and great uncle had died and they feared they probably would not get another chance to meet her before she passed on too. She was getting right up there in years.

Simon had returned with two plates of desserts, one of which he gave to his brother. We fell silent as we enjoyed the desserts and coffee. He had also found a carafe full of coffee for us. When the desserts were gone and coffee cups refilled the conversation continued.

"This morning you mentioned that your grandfather had met Charlie Thomas. Did he ever say anything about Hiram Olson who had been a sheepherder friend of Charlie's?" I asked Ray.

Ray and Simon exchanged looks that reminded me of two kids that had just been caught doing something they weren't supposed to do. Simon told me that his grandfather was kind of acquainted with Crazy Charlie Thomas, mainly through his many stories that he enjoyed. But Charlie hadn't stayed in that country around Idaho Falls very long, so nobody really got to know him very well. Everyone knew he had some kind of problem, but wasn't sure what. Charlie would never talk about it. About the only person that knew Charlie very well was Hiram Olson.

Hiram and Silas had become friends. They spent one season working on the same sheep ranch. Hiram too had a problem that everyone said was because of the combat action he saw during WWII.

Simon went on to tell me about a story his grandfather told about once when he was with Hiram. Hiram had been acting very odd and strangely withdrawn all day. He disappeared; just walked out like he was going to the outdoor toilet, but he never came back. Silas found him that evening sitting on a rock down by the edge of a small runoff creek. He managed to get Hiram back to the little cabin they were sharing and into bed.

Early the next morning just before daybreak Hiram got up and went outside. He shortly returned wearing a large smile and told Silas to be quiet and come with him outside. They stood there for just a few minutes before they heard the howl. It started almost like the bark of a dog; several high pitched barks then it seemed to transform to a long mournful howl ending in a kind of menacing growl. Hiram turned to Silas and said that he knew now that everything would be okay. Seaman had made him better. After a minute's pause he said that he hoped Charlie, wherever he was, had heard Seaman too.

After a bit of silence that gave me time to digest the story Simon had just told I asked why the odd look they exchanged when I first asked about Hiram. Ray said then that earlier they had been talking with a cousin, Emily Keslo. She told them that she had a dog that died several years ago then about a year later he came back to live with her in the reincarnate form of another dog. She said the two dogs looked very different, but the new dog did many things her first dog did. Emily was just starting to get into the details of her story when her father, Earl Keslo, cut in and said her crazy stories were getting tiresome and asked her not to tell any more. Both Ray and Simon were apprehensive to tell the story of Hiram to me because I might consider it to be weird and tiresome.

I assured then it definitely was not weird or tiresome to me, but I would not go into it any more today. I did tell them that I had heard that same bark-howl a few weeks earlier over on the Missouri River in central Montana. In fact that is how I got involved in all this to begin with. It was that bark-howl that had connected me with Crazy Charlie.

That was the short version of my story. But today we all wanted to wander and meet some more of the relatives.

Maybe some time I would stop over to their place in Idaho Falls. I remembered my own father talking about spending time in southern Idaho on a small irrigated farm he rented for several years just before he joined the Army at the outbreak of WW II. I was curious to see the area he had talked about.

12 St. Louis

I had been in St. Louis for several days after the Kelso/Thomas family reunion following leads on the story of Seaman. My notebook was starting to bulge from all the scraps of paper I had written notes on—I still do my field note taking the old fashioned way with paper and pencil. I could see that I had better spend a little time doing some preliminary organizing. If I left everything until I got back home, I probably would not remember what I was trying to say on many of these brief notes scrawled on various scraps of whatever paper was handy.

As I sat there in the small café across from my motel, sipping coffee and reading notes from the pile of papers in front of me, I heard someone calling my name. I looked up, surprised anyone in this city would know me. All of the Keslo/Thomas family had departed by now. Even Kathy had taken a few days off from her café duties. The young man in front of me repeated his inquiry to verify he was indeed talking to the right person.

"Phil Scriver? I am Gary Frosken. My father, Leo Frosken, said you were doing some research on Captain Lewis' dog. He thought he might be able to help. He said that he thought you had come down to the Kelso/Thomas reunion and hoped you might still be hanging around Kathy's café."

"Frosken; I'm sorry but I don't recognize that name. I might know his face, though."

"I didn't think you would know the name or the face. He told me he has never met you, but he has read several of your books and keeps up with your websites. He is an avid Lewis and Clark fan like you."

"Okay, did he want to get together with me sometime, somewhere?"

"Yeah, he asked me to find out what would be convenient for you. He says he is retired so anything would work for him."

"Well I'm just wrapping up my visit here and was thinking about heading out for home. I delay that a while so we have time for a meeting."

"Shall I call my father and have him meet with you here, now?"

"Sure, that would make it easy for me since I'm not very familiar with the city."

"Okay, he only lives a short distance from here. Give me about twenty or thirty minutes to go get him."

"I'll be here. That would give me a little time to work on this pile of notes I have made."

After Gary was gone I dug into the stack of paper in front of me. It was late morning so the breakfast crowd was gone and the lunchtime crowd wouldn't come for a while yet. The place was quiet and there was plenty of good coffee. To me that made for a perfect chance to get some work done.

Most of my effort was spent to expand a few brief words on the scraps of paper into more complete and coherent notes in my notebook for further analysis later. I also needed to do a quick review to be sure I hadn't missed anything I had to follow up on before I left St. Louis. This was the normal mundane work done at the end of every research trip; just tying up loose ends. No new, great revelations were anticipated since I already had a good overview of what I had found.

I was about time Gary had said he would return with his father so I started putting my notes back in their file. My eyes fell on a piece of paper torn from a page of a yellow legal pad. The note on it said *find guy named Leo—don't know last; member of L&C chapter.* Another name on the paper was Laurie Keslo. A smile crossed my face as I thought what a small world. I had tried to get a chance to talk with her at the reunion, but we never quite connected. Everyone at the reunion had wanted to talk with her so the dear lady was kept busy that entire day. I stuffed my notes away, but held out that one. I wanted to make sure the Leo on the note was the same Leo Frosken I would be meeting in a few minutes. Just as I was closing my notebook Gary walked into the café. The older man with him, I presumed, was his father, Leo.

As they approached my table I stood up and extended my hand in greeting, "Good morning. You must be Leo Frosken."

"You must be the guy that's been hearing all those wolves and coyotes."

"I don't know. I've heard my share, but so have a lot of other people."

'Yeah, but you're the one that's going around making a big deal about it."

"Not much of a big deal; just asking some questions cause what I heard was a bit odd; different from anything I had ever heard before."

"I think they are all different depending on where you are and when you heard them."

"You're probably right there. Seems like everyone hears sounds different, especially if they are sounds you are not used to hearing."

"Of course here in the city we don't hear wolves or coyotes. With all the other noise we can hardly hear the dog next door when it barks."

"I suppose the bigger the city the harder it gets for a person to keep up with everything going on."

"It's the same thing all along the river until you get up to South Dakota. There are just so many people anymore that all the wildlife is squeezed out. All a person can hear is city noises."

There was a pause while Leo and his son joined me at my table and the waitress brought more coffee. I continued, "Your son said you had something to tell me."

"I don't know why he came over and dragged me down here. I keep telling him I'm just an old man who is getting forgetful and imagining things."

Gary interrupted with an admonition to his dad that he certainly was a long way from getting forgetful. He reminded his father that "although he was older than the hills" he still knew details that very few others did and that he knew perfectly well what it was that he was anxious to tell me. Gary's comment to his father was answered by silence. It was as if Leo was waiting for me to ask him what was on his mind.

"I have a note here that tells me to find a guy named Leo, don't know the last name, but he is a member of the Lewis and Clark Chapter here. Would you be that Leo" I asked?

"I probably am, but where did you get that" Leo replied, unable to mask the pleased grin on his face?

"I think it was from Kathy. You seem to be a regular at the café here."

"Yeah. I been coming over here from time to time ever since she opened up. Good coffee; her brother roasts it special for her. Great barbecue ribs too."

"Yeah. I got real well acquainted with some one evening in here about a week ago."

The pleasantries were done and Leo became all business. I had apparently passed Leo's test for being sincere. He started talking about a subject that was obviously a huge passion of his, the Lewis and Clark legacy, and Seaman in particular. Although Leo was well into his eighties (I later found out) he was still mentally sharp and soon proved his son was right when he had said Leo knew details very few others knew.

He talked about the days in St. Louis at the time of the Lewis and Clark Expedition's return. That big black dog went everywhere with Lewis. He never let that man out of his sight. It was as if Seaman was his nurse and protector all in one. He knew Lewis was sick and he had to take care of him. Timothy Alden wrote in his 1814 book a few years after Lewis died that nobody knew for sure, but most likely Seaman lay on his master's grave refusing to leave and refusing all offers of food and water until he too perished.

Although it seemed reasonable, that conclusion is simply not true according to Leo. The old timers used to tell the story that after Lewis' death the dog disappeared. For a number of years he would re-appear along the waterfront for several weeks every fall. Sometimes in the early pre-dawn hours a strange howling would be heard. Then he was gone. Spirit Mound was calling him. He was never seen or heard in the area again.

Leo concluded with, "That's all I know about Seaman. But there is a woman by the name of Laurie Keslo that you should talk to. She might be able to tell you more."

"Laurie Keslo" I repeated. "That's funny. I was at the Keslo/Thomas family reunion here a few days ago, but never got a chance to talk with her."

"I heard they was having a big family get together, but I didn't come over to it. I wasn't too sure how well things would go between some of the family. They don't always see eye to eye on things."

"I heard some rumblings of that, but never found out what the disagreement was all about. I guess every family has some that don't get along with others of the family."

"Laurie and I are longtime friends. She is a Lewis and Clark buff like me. In fact she's my next door neighbor. If you want I'll give her a call and see if she wants to come over here and talk with us. That is if you have time."

"I've got all the time in the world," I assured Leo. "Somehow Seaman has been taking all my time for several months now ever since I heard that strange bark-howl on the cliffs above the Missouri River."

It wasn't long before Laurie walked into the café and spying Leo, Gary and I, she came straight over to our table.

"Good morning Leo. What brings you out so early? It isn't even noon yet."

"I've just been talking with a guy here that I think you should meet."

When the introductions were made Laurie acknowledged that Scott had told her about me and, although she knew I was at the reunion, they all kept her too busy. She hadn't been given a chance to meet me. When Leo had called her she hadn't hesitated in coming over to the café to talk with me. Scott had told her about my search for Seaman and she had some information to pass on that she was sure I would be interested in.

Laurie started by telling me that she considered Scott to be her grandson because she has raised his father, Willie, from the time he was five when his mother had died. She had never met Willie's father, Charlie Thomas, but knew he was out there somewhere, roaming the country, unable to settle down in one place for very long.

Many years ago she had talked with her brothers in Idaho about Charlie. When they told her about his problems she developed a kind of a soft spot for him in her heart. That bit of knowledge helped her understand Willie in later years. They had also talked about his only real friend, Hiram Olson. Hiram had some problems like Charlie, but he seemed to be handling his problems better. Her brothers also told her about Seaman and hearing his bark-howl. Hiram told them it was Seaman making him get better. Her brothers described the bark-howl just like the old timers had described what they had heard along the waterfront in St. Louis in the years following Lewis' death. They swore it was Seaman.

Leo interrupted her to say he had told me the stories about Seaman being seen along the waterfront after Lewis died. He also had told me about Alden's 1814 book and his wrong conclusion about Seaman's death.

Laurie agreed that the conclusion was not true then continued her story. When Willie came to live with her and her husband their only son, Earl, never liked him. To this day he thinks both Willie and his father, Charlie Thomas, were two of a kind. Both were worthless and never contributed much of anything to society. He steadfastly believes they were more than just a little crazy. It still hurt Laurie that her two "kids" never got along. She speculated that Earl was jealous of Willie because he had been an only child. When Willie came along Earl had to share his mother and father with his new brother. He probably was more resentful because Willie was not a good student or particularly well liked. He was more of a loner and not good at socializing even as a young boy. Earl was just the opposite. Although he never said anything about it, Laurie was sure that other kids in school tormented Earl about his weird brother.

Even though he would never admit it Earl and Willie had several things in common. Both of them had been in the military and had served in Vietnam. Earl had been a pilot and flew uncountable number of missions in various parts of the country without any mishaps. Some of his missions were over very dangerous areas while others were very mundane, but as he told people any and every mission in a theater of war is potentially deadly.

Willie had been in the infantry. His first tour had been early in the war and he was in some of the tough fighting where American forces took heavy casualties. He came home from Vietnam and got out of the Army. Try as he would he could not adjust to civilian life. After about a year of almost continual trouble with the law and never being able to keep a job Willie went back into the Army and was soon assigned to a second tour in Vietnam. He was killed in combat just a few months later.

Laurie told us that they were all thankful that he never got re-involved with his wife and son during that year he was in St. Louis and out of the Army. He would have only caused them more hardship and grief than they already had to deal with. She said most of the family was convinced he went back into the Army because he knew he would be sent to Vietnam. His death in combat somewhere in the jungles of Vietnam was his way of committing suicide. He knew he was getting deeper and deeper into trouble with the law and his personal problems just kept growing more out of control. That was the only way he could see to resolve his problems.

Laurie's story was followed by a time of silence as everyone digested what had been said. Finally, almost apologetically, Laurie told us that it was very odd to hear someone say Willie had committed suicide, even if it did come from her own mouth. She had thought it for a long time, but never said so before.

I told Laurie that I had some brothers and several close friends who had served in Vietnam. They all said that "combat suicide" was not uncommon over there. It was kind of standard procedure to watch guys who were serving second and third tours closely to guard against them needlessly exposing themselves to the enemy as a method of committing suicide.

After a bit more general chatter as we finished our coffee, we said our goodbyes and I headed to the airport to catch my flight home.

13 A Mind Out of Control

On the flight home I couldn't help thinking more about the story Laurie had told about Willie and his father, Charlie.

PTSD is a very spooky thing. Although I had spent time in the military and had seen some very limited combat I decided I was very thankful that I didn't have the problems that some of the people I had been hearing about. I have known a number of other people who also had been in the military who did not show any of the signs of PTSD. My fear was giving way to curiosity. I had read that PSTD is an avoidance mechanism the mind uses when a person feels they are very vulnerable to something beyond their control and they are no longer safe and secure. What made the difference that some people were affected and others were not? Maybe I should do some more research about that aspect of the ailment.

I was certain that three people were victims of PTSD. What I wanted to know is why each one dealt with their disability so differently. Hiram had basically learned to overcome his. He got it under control many years before I talked with him. Charlie never got a good control on his disorder until near the end of his life. Charlie's son, Willie, apparently was unable to do anything to control his problems. He decided the only way he could overcome his disorder was to end his life.

I had no clue if Will Tanner ever suffered with PTSD since dementia or Alzheimer's had almost completely taken over his mind. Nobody I had talked with ever said much of anything about Will. He appeared to have simply been one of herders in Idaho and later left for a life on his farm in North Dakota.

As soon as I got home I sat down to my computer, bypassing the chores of catching up on my emails I had received, and went straight to google to read more about post traumatic stress. There were still too many unanswered questions running through my mind for me to be comfortable.

The websites I visited told me that the severity of PTSD and the individual's ability to overcome the disorder depend on a variety of factors. An active, optimistic, out-going person generally has better success dealing with and overcoming PTSD than does the more introverted, pessimistic person. But other factors such as the person's social network, support group or circle of friends and family modify that recovery model.

Two techniques that have been used for overcoming PTSD, even before it was known as a mental disorder, is having a pet dog and having a friend or friends that the person can talk about it with. This was the forerunner to the concept of support group.

Of course getting professional help is the most important aspect of recovery. As society successfully changes from the "General Patton" perspective to the current day realization that PTSD is a potentially deadly or severly debilitating mental illness, those that suffer PTSD will find much more complete recovery.

The cure sounds so simple but any time you are dealing with the human mind there is really nothing that is simple about it. As a person comes to terms with what caused the trauma and overcomes the feelings of helplessness recovery is under way. In generations passed people with PTSD were never allowed the opportunities find a cure or complete recovery. The lucky ones at best found a way to control its effects.

I could now see that the extensive deaths and destruction Willie had witnessed had thoroughly overcome him. He had absolutely no support group- friends, family, etc. to help him. Inevitably, his "survivor's guilt" engulfed him causing Willie to commit suicide.

The website went on to say other factors like severity of the event, how long it lasted, and if it was an intentional, man-made event and the person may even have been subjected to multiple events. While many different happenings can cause PTSD the ravages of war have long been recognized as the most severe cause of the disorder because of its widespread impact on so many people. Some say that no one who has been in actual combat can walk away without any scars or some measure of post-traumatic stress.

It has only been realized in more recent years that the other events should be included as causing PTSD. Most every adverse event includes a period of PTSD. It is a normal reaction to the event. However, almost everyone will overcome the stress and resume a normal life. The death of a loved one and the period of grieving are often used as typical examples.

Today psychiatrists look at two other areas to understand PTSD, pre-event and post-event. Pre-event considers family history of violence and family support. They try to determine how the person grew up and formed his mental make-up. Post-event includes the person's social network beyond the family and mental toughness, his will to get better, to see if he might learn to cope with the adversities of the event.

One of the very common symptoms of PTSD is avoiding the place the event happened. Consequently recovery will frequently hinge on being able to visit that place again without setting off adverse reactions. These reactions are usually termed "flashbacks" and can also happen just "out of the blue" without visiting the scene. This exposure therapy is helpful, but it can easily be missed if the person is the type that hide his reactions by controlling his inner emotions. Depression and emotional numbness are basic PTSD symptoms that must be overcome for the person to recover.

Other methods used to overcome PTSD are to be involved in things that tend to be pleasant and relaxing such as hiking and camping and other recreational activities in nature. Pets, particularly dogs, are very helpful since they tend to make the person relax and let their internal guard down as they learn to trust again. This is sometimes considered the first step in putting the trauma in the past and realizing it over.

I thought that by now I had a reasonable understanding of PTSD, for a layman, but there were still questions floating around in my mind that were wanting answers.

Questions like how was Seaman tied to PTSD? I could understand Seaman visiting Charlie and Hiram. According to what Hiram had told me he visited people with problems, presumably those with PTSD. I don't know how Seaman searching for his master tied to people with PTSD. Leo Frosken had told me the old timers in St. Louis said Seaman never let Lewis out of his sight. It was as if the dog knew his master was sick with malaria and he had to take care of him. Maybe somehow he equated the deliriums Lewis had with malaria with the devastating flashbacks of PTSD sufferers.

Why had I heard Seaman? Although I spent time in the military and saw some very limited combat I surely did not suffer from PTSD. I was certainly well beyond any adverse effects of that type my military life might have had on me.

Why did he visit my sister's farm? People may think that she is a little weird for wanting to live a solitary life on her farm rather than mixing with the crowds of the city, but I don't think that qualifies for PTSD. There was no great event that happened to her to make her withdraw from the world. She simply preferred to continue the more solitary farm life she grew up with.

How did Seaman cure both Hiram and Crazy Charlie? They both told me he had. What unique healing powers did Seaman have? Dogs are sometimes used today as pets for PTSD sufferers as a part of the recovery process, but neither Hiram nor Charlie spent extended periods of time with Seaman like they would have with a pet. Although dogs are a useful part of the recovery process from what I have read I don't believe that most people would credit dogs with healing anyone with PTSD.

I felt like I had hit a wall that was proving to be too high to climb over and too long to get around. The time had come for me to set this all aside and let it mellow for a while.

The bark-howl I had heard was the same sound Charlie and Hiram had heard. Dan's grandfather and both of Laurie's brothers in Idaho had heard it just as the early day folks in St. Louis had described the sound. But how could it be possible since these instances covered a two hundred year span of time? I had hoped that my trip to the reunion would give me some answers to help solve the Seaman puzzle. Instead my head just seemed to be crammed with more questions that needed to have answers found.

14 Believers

I was just puttering around in my basement office, telling myself that I was busy straightening and organizing my notes on Seaman, but my mind was somewhere else. I felt so totally worn out mentally from reading through all my notes again and trying to understand them, with very little success. It was like trying to put together a giant jigsaw puzzle. Maybe if I put some things in a different order it would all make better sense. I had tried that several times already but nothing I did produced any results.

For some reason Emily Keslo entered my thoughts. I remembered her story about her dog that died. She was certain that it came back into her life in a reincarnate for of another dog. It hadn't meant much of anything to me at the time Ray had told me about it during the family reunion, but now it put my mind into high gear. This was an area I had not thought about or explored at all until now. I am not sure if I was now just grasping at straws or not, but I remember many years ago I had read a book written by a guy who had worked with a woman and helped her remember several past lives. The book made a very strong case for reincarnation.

Since that time I had never really thought much more about it. I know some people felt very strongly that reincarnation was real, but most others I knew either did not believe it existed or simply ignored the subject.

Maybe this was the next path I needed to follow. It was time to fire up my computer and go visit google.

When I googled reincarnation I got a long list of sites about the Hindu religion. I dutifully transcribed notes on Hinduism and their beliefs about reincarnation. I might have a few more pieces to the puzzle, but I couldn't see what they were.

I did learn that Hinduism is a collection of many religious sects or groups and is considered to be the world's oldest religion. It ranks number three in number of followers. The essence of my notes was the fifth basic belief of Hinduism. "The soul reincarnates, revolving through many births until all karmas have been resolved and moksha is attained. Karma is defined as our acts or deeds and moksha is the liberation from the cycle of rebirths.

It is important to understand Hindus believe reincarnation is the maturing of our soul since we are at any given time a sum total of all our past lives. Through the series of rebirths there may be, from time to time, a rebirth in animal form.

I realized that I had spent several hours reading about the Hindu religion and general beliefs. I even read some accounts of people relating past lives and others conducting séances to speak to departed family members.

After reading a great deal more about Hinduism than I ever imagined I would, I clicked out of google. I doubted that any more information on Hindu religious beliefs was going to get me any closer to solving the Seaman riddle.

I returned to google and looked up animal reincarnation just to see what I could find. To my surprise I read that the ancient Greek and Egyptian civilizations believed in reincarnation of animals. The website I was reading added Buddhists and Hindus to the list of believers.

A commonly held belief was that the soul's karma growth frequently included animal forms, particularly in the earlier stages. They also said that animals may return in the same animal form several times before eventually being reborn as another animal or as a human.

They are reborn into the same animal form several times until their purpose for living has been completed, then they pass to a new life form for a new purpose and the cycle is repeated. An animal can, and often does, exhibit characteristics unique to his new life as well as some that are common to his old life. According to the believers this is how the animal says his purpose for being on earth has not yet been completed.

This philosophy from animal reincarnation believers is very much like the Hindu's fifth basic belief in the growth of a human soul's karma until it reaches moksha. Hindu's agree that animal rebirths can take place during that process.

To my surprise one web site I read reported that several surveys have been taken that show at least sixty percent of all the American people believe in the concept of reincarnation. Some tie it to the concept of predestination—everything happens for a reason—while others do not go that far.

Many of the "animal reincarnation" hits were difficult to separate the religion aspects from general belief. Just like the Hindu and Buddhist religions, they included their belief in reincarnation. The only differences were the reasons why it occurs. Most non-religion sites seemed to say that not every person or animal is reincarnated. Reincarnation was the result of some kind of a need.

Many of the 16,000 "animal reincarnation" hits were testimonials to prove a pet had returned in the form of another animal. They were primarily dealing with cats and dogs, but a few horses were included too. Reasons why the pet was reincarnated were usually not given, only that it happened.

I wished that I had been able to talk with Emily and ask her if she had any thoughts on why her dog and returned in another life form. Maybe she would have some clues as to its unfinished work.

One site I found was written by a woman who had devoted twenty years to research on animal life after death and returning to earth in a new form. She says animal communicators can talk to departed animals. They explain the connection of past and future lives as "sometimes all the efforts in the world will not completely resolve an issue in one lifetime. Sometimes it can take several lifetimes to learn everything or cure a problem. She never gave any examples of what kinds of problems may be left unfinished.

During my reading I found this statement that was simply credited as a Buddhist philosophy. "A large proportion of human suffering occurs because people think they only live once. When they become fully aware that the present life is only one point in the eternal flow of time and that they have lived in the past and will live again in the future, they will understand that their future lives will depend on their present life."

I had absolutely no idea why I copied that particular quote. I could see no way it helped me solve my puzzle. I guess I just kind of liked what it had to say. Besides it sounded mysterious and showed how this whole reincarnation thing is based on beliefs and not necessarily facts.

At last I clicked out of google. I decided that I had read enough from believers in animal reincarnation. I was at least partly convinced it might happen, but I still was no closer to understanding my puzzle than I had been that morning before I started reading all the reincarnation websites. Everything I had read seemed like it was based on belief and had no facts to support or prove their basic contentions. I still could not prove Seaman had been visiting people along the Missouri River.

I was almost to the point of giving up and saying it was only my imagination what I had "heard" that morning on the cliffs above the river. If people wanted to believe Seaman was running around the country who was I to argue with them? I didn't have the necessary proof to empirically agree or disagree.

But several succeeding generations of people over a two hundred year period had described that bark-howl in almost exactly the same words without ever knowing about the earlier descriptions. A little voice inside me kept reminding me that I had actually heard that bark-howl I described, and it was not just my imagination. My description was exactly the same as all the others had been ever since his days on the St. Louis waterfront.

I didn't feel like I was any closer to fitting the puzzle pieces together. Maybe it was just the opposite. Maybe I was farther away because I found I had more pieces than I had before.

15 Hiram's Last Feast

When Hiram had written to me about keeping his notebooks he had mentioned in the letter that he was arranging a feast with some of the Sioux elders. It was to be held on his farm down by the Cannonball River in the same place they had many feasts over the years. He said he would let me know the details later when they had all been worked out. Consequently I was not surprised to get a letter with a return address on it for the Sioux tribe on the Standing Rock reservation.

When I tore open the letter and started to read it I stopped and just stared at it in disbelief. I had to sit down to finish the letter. Hiram had just passed away. Although I had actually just met him one time, that meeting along with the time I spent reading his notebooks made it seem like he was a close friend and I had known him for a long time. As the old cliché goes, inside his gruff, rough-tough exterior was a truly warm and caring person who was easy to get to know. His memoirs had shown me a man who was deeply concerned for all things around him, but in life he just couldn't quite overcome is fears of being torn apart by unknown factors he was unable to control. Maybe he had hidden behind that rough cover for so long he just couldn't let it go.

I finally returned my full attention to the letter in my hands. It was written by the tribe's cultural minister who suggested to me that the feast Hiram had been arranging should be held as planned, but it should be Hiram's wake. Most of Hiram's friends were tribal members and he had no family that anyone in Bismarck knew about. With my concurrence the wake would be set for a date just two days off and would be held on Hiram's farm. Since it was to be held outside they wanted to do it before the weather turned bad.

We were still experiencing warm sunny afternoons, probably our last few before winter set in, so I emailed a quick reply that I would be there. I packed a quick duffel bag and prepared for an early morning departure. The plan was for me to meet one of the elders at Hiram's place in Bismarck where I would spend the night. From there I could go down to Hiram's farm for the wake then stay there a few days or return to Bismarck, whichever I wanted.

Things went as planned and I spent the following night at Hiram's place in Bismarck. I called the cultural minister, Harvey Wells, as I had been told and we headed out to Hiram's farm 80 miles away. As we rolled into the farm yard we saw no other vehicles had arrived.

"Typical" Harvey mumbled to himself but loud enough for me to hear. Almost apologetically he explained to me, "All of the elders are quite old and have to depend on others to get everything ready. But nobody seems to be doing anything. Looks like maybe you and I should get things going."

"I'm game for whatever we need to do" I told him.

"Good, let's see if we have enough stuff here to cook up a feast. We will only prepare enough for the elders, probably six, plus you and me. The others probably will not come since the elders didn't invite anyone."

"All right let's see if there is any wood cut for a fire. We can probably cut some small saplings down by the river to make a tripod to hang the food over the fire to cook."

"What shall we eat beside the antelope we shoot" Harvey asked me?

"Has one already been shot" I asked?

"No. I can't see well enough any more to do any hunting."

"Okay. It's a good piece of luck I brought my old 30-06 with me. I haven't used it for several years, but I can still hit what I aim at with it."

"That's good since I have given all my guns away to my sons and grandsons. I can't use them anymore."

"What else are we going to have to eat?"

"I will make some berry soup."

"How about bread or potatoes or vegetables?"

"I don't know anything about fixing any of that stuff over a campfire."

"I used to do historic re-enacting of the Lewis and Clark Expedition. I was a cook so we will have a Corps of Discovery supper special. Can we get some flour somewhere close by?"

"We can go in to Porcupine. That's not far from here. It is on the way to where we can go shoot an antelope."

We poked around Hiram's place and found a modest supply of wood cut and split; enough for a good campfire. We also found a bucket and rope to tie a tripod together and to hang the bucket over the fire. We cut three poles about two inches in diameter and six feet long for our tripod.

With these initial preparations completed it was time to get the antelope shot and purchase a few other items for the feast. At my invitation Harvey climbed into my Ford pickup and we headed off for Porcupine.

After a quick fifteen mile trip we pulled up to a rundown looking building that served as the town's gas station, grocery store, restaurant, bar and post office. Harvey started talking with two young guys who had pulled up just behind us. I went inside and made my way over to the grocery shelves where I found a sack of flour and several bottles of cooking oil. I allowed myself the luxury of purchasing a can of coffee. Our feast was going to be an historically accurate Lewis and Clark Expedition meal with food prepared as they would have in 1804—almost. But I knew from reading the Expedition's journals that they drank coffee during the winter they spent camped near Bismarck at Fort Mandan.

When I came out of the store Harvey was waiting for me in my pickup. He explained to me that the two young men he had talked with were going to take us out to where they had seen some antelope earlier in the day. They figured that by using both vehicles we could run down an antelope for us.

At that point I interrupted and told Harvey that all I wanted was for them to get me to the area where the antelope were. I never chase down antelope to shoot them because the meat tastes terribly "goaty" when they get hot from being run. I knew a better way to get a close, clean shot and avoid running the animals. I assured them that I had shot many antelope using the method I was going to use today. When antelope are shot this way they actually taste better than deer. I told them when I was a kid growing up on the prairies of central Montana antelope was a big part of our family's meat supply. I had killed my fair share. With everyone in agreement we headed out. The young guys were curious as to what I was going to do.

We went a few miles out of Porcupine then turned northeast off the dirt road we had been following. We were now just driving across the prairie. Out here there was no such thing as roads. We had traveled several miles in the direction of some distant hills when the two guys in front stopped. We got out of our pickups and gazed across the landscape as one of the young men showed us where the antelope had been grazing that morning. We walked about a half mile to the crest of a small hill. As we scanned the valley below, we could see several antelope lying in the grass.

We crawled back down the hill to plan our strategy. It was too far to make a good shot so we had to get closer. The antelope were lying closer to the hills on the other side of the valley so we would need to get over there for a much closer shot.

We decided we would walk back to our pickups and make a large loop to the east staying downwind and out of sight of the antelope. Eventually we would get to the hills on the other side of the valley. I would then drive a stake in the ground and tie a white cloth on it. When that was done I would move a short distance away from the flag and wait. Although they were lying down those antelope were also watching everything around them very carefully so they would soon see my flag. Antelope, being very curious animals, can't resist and will come investigate the strange thing they see. I have seen them walk up and sniff the flag waving in the southwest breeze, totally ignoring me lying a mere 25 feet away. I have shot several antelope this way. I have also got many close-up photos this same way by taking advantage of the natural antelope curiosity. I prefer this over the long telephoto lenses that always distort a photo a bit.

Today the plan worked to perfection. Within a half hour from the time I tied my flag on the stake in the ground we had the antelope we would be eating a little later. Almost the same time my shot rang out two more shots from my young guides dropped more antelope. As soon as the animals were on the ground our young men were on them. I knew the fun was over and the work was beginning so I willingly let them do that part of the job.

The years of practice showed as they quickly field-dressed and skinned the animals. I told them I wanted the butterfly steaks that lie along the backbone in the tenderloin area. They were welcome to take the rest of the animals for themselves, including the skins. In no time at all the guys had the butchering completed and the meat loaded. They also had the hides loaded and the innards left out where the coyotes would find them as soon as we departed. That's the interesting thing about coyotes. A person never sees them around, but as soon as you leave an area coyotes are there to investigate and clean up any food scraps that may have been left.

It was late afternoon when we pulled into the farm yard at Hiram's place. Several other vehicles were there telling us the elders of the tribe were gathering for Hiram's wake. We still had time to get the campfire going and the food cooking. Even after the sun went down the campfire would keep us plenty warm for several more hours.

Harvey got a good fire going while I prepared the food for cooking. In no time we had a bucket of oil hung over the fire and a kettle of water heating to cook some squash in. Our activity attracted the attention of the elders who soon joined us at the campfire.

Curiosity that day was not limited to just the antelope. The elders couldn't resist directing questions at whoever would answer. Where is the meat and isn't it late to start cooking a roast over a campfire? Where is the other food for our feast?

While I went about my tasks of cooking our feast Harvey talked with the elders. He told the assembled group what we were going to have to eat and how we would cook it. When he said it was all being done as the Lewis and Clark Expedition had done it two hundred years earlier everyone was impressed and pleased. Someone gave me a hand and took the coffee into the farm house and made a much-appreciated pot while we were getting the other things ready.

We soon had the bucket of cooking oil (the Expedition would have used animal fat but we didn't have any) hot enough to just start to boil. As everyone watched in great curiosity I deftly slipped several of the butterfly steaks into the oil. As they started cooking I put several pieces of flattened bread dough into the oil also. Three minutes later the bread and antelope steaks were scooped out of the oil with a long-handled spoon, ready to eat. The Expedition cooked their foods in oil. Today we call it deep fat frying. Harvey's wife appeared with a stack of plates that she placed on a low table, and then disappeared, returning quickly with a pan of boiled squash. She had taken the liberty of cooking it inside on the kitchen stove while she had also been keeping us supplied with coffee.

I continued cooking the antelope meat and bread in the boiling oil while the others got brave enough to sample the feast; antelope steak, bread, squash and coffee. Soon all the talk died as everyone ate their fill of this simple, but tasty food that was made better by feasting in the great outdoors around the campfire. Hiram had nailed it when he mentioned those feasts he had in years gone by "good food, good talk, good friends".

When I had finished my cooking duties and we had all eaten our fill, I rose a gave each person a shot of the remains of a bottle of Wild Turkey whiskey I had found at Hiram's place in Bismarck. We drank a toast to Hiram Olson.

Several long minutes of silence followed. I wasn't sure if people were reflecting on Hiram and their time spent with him or if the spell of the day had been broken and everyone was just waiting for an excuse to go home.

At length someone related a brief story about an incident he remembered with Hiram. That story soon lead to another and another. Everyone was freely sharing their most treasured stories of experiences with Hiram. Before we realized it the fire had been left unattended so long it was about out and we were all getting chilled. Harvey and I found a supply of wood and got the fire going again. With the renewed warmth the stories continued until the sun started making its journey across the sky.

The bright sun prodded us into action. It was time to get home to breakfast and some sleep. None of us were accustomed to staying up all night.

I decided to stay at the farm a while; just poke around before I headed back to Bismarck to wrap up his burial and estate. I told myself that I needed to have a better idea of what was left on the farm to consider for estate matters. I also needed to look through the house in case anything had been left there that I needed to know about.

I knew deep down it was my way of saying goodbye to Hiram. It was still strange to me that a person I had only met one time had become so close to me.

16. Rest in Peace

I poked around the farm yard and in the shop enough to satisfy my curiosity and ensure that there was nothing of consequence lying around. Hiram had not farmed the place for a number of years so most everything of any value or usefulness had been sold or had "walked off" over time. Even the pile of scrap iron every farm accumulates over the years had been hauled away.

I made my way into the house where to my pleasure I discovered there was enough coffee left to brew a pot. I spent the next couple of hours carefully searching the house to be sure nothing had been left there that I needed to remove and deal with separately from the farm. From the odds and ends of food and a few blankets I found I decided someone used the place from time to time, but it didn't look like any damage had been done and it had been kept clean. It could have been Hiram using it, but I suspected others since it was a two hour drive from Bismarck and at Hiram's age I didn't think he would make the trip very often.

After I had satisfied myself that everything was in order I washed up the dishes we had used for our feast along with a few strays I found. With that done I carefully locked the house, returning the key to its hiding place everyone knew, and headed out to Bismarck.

As I drove along I decided the first thing I needed to do was to get some food and some sleep. I would then spend the next few days examining Hiram's house and getting his estate in order. Another idea was forming in my mind. Unless I found something to the contrary, I was thinking Hiram would be cremated and I would scatter his ashes at his farm on the Cannonball River.

The sound of the grandfather clock tolling out 7:00 pm woke me. It took several long seconds for me to remember where I was. I fumbled around in the dark living room until I found the switch to a table lamp close by. I wasn't entirely sure if I had been dreaming or just remembering what had been told to me by the elders, but I had to write it down. I would figure out where it came from later.

The Little Devils that lived on Spirit Mound jealously guarded their kingdom from all intruders. The people who lived in the area had come to know only too well that their sharp pointed arrows were deadly and the Little Devils did not hesitate to shoot them. As a result only an occasional incursion to Spirit Mound was made, almost always with tragic results.

When Captains Meriwether Lewis and William Clark decided to go investigate the Mound they were warned against doing so.

First, Lewis noticed that his chronometer stopped just after he set it the morning they were to go to Spirit Mound. Lewis apparently tried to fix it, but he gave up with a comment stating the fix was beyond his abilities. Days later he reported using it again so it somehow started working again after they were passed the home of the Little Devils.

But the Captains and the men didn't heed that warning. They were all determined to go see the Spirit Mound they had been told about. They doubted the story they had been told.

During their walk to the Mound they became extremely hot and thirsty. These men who were well accustomed to physical labors all day long also became very tired. This was the Little Devils second warning not to invade their kingdom. Others who had tried to set foot on the kingdom of the Little Devils in the past were alone or a very small group. The Little Devils easily dispatched them, but the group with the Captains was large and well-armed so other action would be necessary.

All the Little Devils turned themselves into birds so they could keep a watch over these invaders, but not be attacked. When the large black dog became overheated causing the men to send him back, the Little Devils had their opening. Alone he was no match for the many sharp arrows that struck him.

The grand ceremony that followed separated Seaman's physical body from his spirit. The feast provided the Little Devils a much-needed renewal of both their physical and spiritual strengths. Seaman's spirit was placed into a new physical form to rejoin Captain Lewis. His new duty would be to wander the western waterways searching for his departed master. As he wandered he had to help others in their times of great need.

It was almost midnight by the time I got the Spirit Mound legend completed. I couldn't quite remember if I had eaten anything, but right then a good bed was all I wanted. I would get busy on Hiram's estate in the morning.

For the next week I carefully went through the house cleaning out personal stuff, inventorying furnishings, and all the other details of disposing of the house and farm. I talked with an estate lawyer and found out that, in the absence of any other legal papers that contradicted or superseded it, Hiram's letter asking me to take care of his estate would suffice for a will and gave me complete prerogative to do as I wished with everything, including keeping it all if I so desired. The only exception was that the state historical society was to receive all left over cash.

I called Harvey Wells and discussed the farm with him. My intention was to give the tribe Hiram's farm, along with his Ford Ranger and all other items around the farmstead. I had discovered Hiram had sold all the land but the few acres the farm house and outbuildings occupied so it wasn't a large windfall, but

I suspected the area was important to the collective memories.

Harvey and the elders were very pleased to get the farm because Hiram had been a special person to them for many years. There had been many feasts over the years where we held the wake. I found out this place on the banks of the Cannonball River was highly prized by them.

When I contacted the North Dakota State Historical Society they said they knew Hiram Olson. He had given several talks at Society sponsored events. Although he had never become a member of the Society, over the years he had regularly given them cash contributions. They were excited to learn of my plans to give the Society Hiram's house and its contents. I told them, as I had also told the tribe, that my lawyer would be working with them to complete the details of the gift. They could keep or sell any or all of the gift, as they saw fit.

My last item of business was to scatter Hiram's ashes. Earlier in the week I had talked with the funeral home and completed arrangements for them to cremate Hiram. I had found in Hiram's personal papers that he had prepaid for his funeral. He was to be cremated, but he had not purchased a cemetery plot. I had informed the funeral home that I would be taking the ashes and scattering them on his farm so not plot was required.

When I had talked with Harvey about the farm I told him that I would be scattering the ashes. One of the elders wanted to help me with the ceremony. He was almost begging, saying he and Hiram had been very close, almost brothers, for many years and scattering his ashes at the sacred Cannonball River was the greatest honor he could bestow on Hiram. Harvey told me this story.

"When Hiram first came to the Cannonball country and was trying to establish his farm a young Indian boy by the name of Johnny Little Crow came to see what this stranger was doing. All the man had was an old sheepwagon for a house. He had been there for several weeks slowly clearing the rocks and brush by hand from an area of several acres. It didn't look like the poor man had very much to eat. Little Crow brought with him a freshly killed antelope as a gift of friendship. This was the first feast held at Hiram's farm. Over the years many more followed. They were always small and very personal rituals between close friends. That is why we had to have antelope for Hiram's wake.

Harvey finished his story by saying that Johnny Little Crow is the main elder of the tribe today. He was the elder that had told me the legend of Spirit Mound.

With the estate matters settled and Hiram's funeral taken care of, my duties in Bismarck were completed and it was time for me to get back home. I had acquired several more pieces to the Seaman puzzle and wanted to try to fit them all into place.

17 Afterward

When I got home from Bismarck I decided I would take a break and just let the events of the last few months gel. Things had been moving fast and I felt I needed to slow them down a bit. I sure didn't want to miss some important details.

Research takes on many forms and can be one of the most interesting aspects of writing. Research obviously includes searching through old papers in archives of all kinds. But that is greatly reduced by computers, particularly for fiction writers and essayists. Google is a godsend.

But the real enjoyment in research is the visits to locations and talking to people. When I want to be sure my location descriptions are good, I take a trip and see what the place actually looks like. How could a person who has never seen miles of constantly moving desert sands write about it, beyond maybe a brief mention of its existence? The visits are enjoyable, but they can get very tiring.

While I was recovering from my Bismarck activities I decided I would see about getting Hiram's memoirs ready for publication. I hired a data entry person with specific instructions of absolutely no editing. Do not change a word, or even a comma, of the text Hiram had written. I impressed upon her that it was his memoirs and he was no longer alive to agree to any changes. I made sure to tell her about the mess she would find in the story about Hiram's feasts and it was critical to get it exactly as he had written it. With an easy smile she assured me she would prepare a digital version of precisely what was on the paper documents I had given her.

I took the photo album to a local firm that did high resolution scanning. The process of getting all of Hiram's photos converted would take some time. They were an important element of his overall story so they had to be the best we could get them.

After some debate with myself I decided I would wrap a prologue and epilogue around Hiram's writings explaining what he did and how I came to publish it. The epilogue would be a few of the stories that had been told at his final feast on the Cannonball River.

The pages of Hiram's scribbling that I had pulled from the memoirs were still lying on my desk. I had decided not to include them in the main text of the book. I wanted to deal with them in the introduction. Hopefully I could get some good photos of a few of the pages to show readers what he had done.

Working the details of getting "Hiram's Notebook" ready for publication occupied me for the next several weeks, but I had all the text and scanned photos, with Hiram's captions, laid out and ready to go to print. All that remained to be done was for me to write my prologue and epilogue. I was pleased with what I had.

The epilogue would be fairly straight forward to do. It would start with a few short paragraphs summarizing Hiram's life. Following that would be a few short stories. I had recorded several stories at the last feast that I planned to use. All of the storytellers had agreed to allow me to use them. In fact, they were pleased that I was including them in Hiram's book.

I was unsettled with how to handle the prologue. After several failed attempts I realized the only way I was going to get anything was just tell the story of how I met Hiram from start to end. That approach would lead to how I came to read the notebooks and the discussion of the scribblings. I would end with a bittersweet comment on the memoirs adding to our knowledge of the era and showing how far we have come, but how far we still have to go until we fully understand mental disease.

With the plan of how to proceed decided upon, I dived headlong into my writing. Before I realized it, I had completed both the prologue and epilogue. After adding them to the memoirs "Hiram's Notebook" was on its way to the publisher.

It felt good to have "Hiram's Notebook"—I had decided on that name for his book—done. I was certain that it was cause for a few days rest and a chance for me to do nothing that involved any thought. I did not want to even turn on my computer. This was to be my time to finally get caught up on some little jobs around the house I had been putting off—my wife says some had been for several years.

My plans worked well for three days then Seaman invaded my mind again. It started innocently enough. I remember smiling at myself as I thought about Hiram's feasts.

Feasts were a common thread to understanding the Seaman story. The thread started with the Sioux legends of Spirit Mound and the Little Devils. Hiram continues it with his many feasts on the farm by the Cannonball River. The feasts covered almost half a century from the time a young Sioux brought an antelope to feed a starved-looking man trying to clear enough land to start a farm and ending with that man's wake on that same farm after his death.

One of the most garbled stories Hiram wrote in his memoirs was when he tried to talk about the feasts. Apparently the most important one was the most difficult one. Maybe Seaman was guarding his secret.

My mind dropped that thought and jumped to another aspect of the story. Maybe Seaman showed himself to me to enlist me into his work to help others in need—with PTSD—by telling their stories like I had just done for Hiram.

But why me? There are many other writers that could tell the story with much greater eloquence. My mind drifted off that question? I had asked myself that many times before. The only answer I found was "it is what it is."

I got lost further in thought. Maybe PTSD is the real story I am dealing with. Maybe I am supposed to be helping Seaman with the mission given to him by the Little Devils as punishment for invading Spirit Mound.

I had three brothers who probably had PTSD. I never realized it until now. One brother returned from hard combat in Vietnam to spend his time getting drunk, or recovering from a hangover by getting drunk again. After several car wrecks, two of which should have killed him, he caused a multi-car pile-up that sent a family of five to intensive care. They lay near death for several weeks while my brother somehow managed to recover from his own injuries. When he left the hospital one of the nurses told him that he had been in such bad condition when the ambulance brought him in that none of them ever thought they would see him leave the hospital alive.

The local state highway patrol trooper took him to see the harm he had caused. When my brother saw the three little kids, all under five years old, in a coma and being kept alive by the machines hooked to them he threw up on the floor then collapsed and passed out from the shock of what he saw.

That incident seemed to give him the mental strength to eventually overcome alcohol and get his PTSD under control. He lived a normal life since then. He got married and raised two kids of his own.

Another brother was also involved in heavy fighting in Vietnam. He spent two years with a Green

Beret team witnessing constant death and destruction all around him. When he finally got back home we all quickly learned not to surprise him or make loud noises that could in any way resemble war sounds. He had learned during his time in combat that the best defense is a strong offense. He would probably hurt someone who surprised him.

His return and recuperation seemed to go well and his PTSD was short-lived. He did have a hard time staying in one place very long before moving on, but that trait had been well defined long before his war experiences. He just seemed to be like a number of his other older relatives and had a compelling urge to see what other places looked like. He often said he was just born to wander.

My third brother had never been thought to have any mental problems. After I had done some research on PTSD I came to realized that PTSD can result from many causes beyond war. This brother was normal, friendly with many people, and did well in school until some time after my father sold the farm and we moved to town.

We did not detect anything in particular at the time, but over the years as he grew to adulthood he seemed to withdraw from everything until he simply disappeared. Several years later he was found living a survivalist/mountain man life on a mountainside in Idaho. Several members of the family tried to talk with him without success. He again disappeared and has never been heard from again. We think he is in Alaska, but who knows? He may not even be alive.

I wondered if maybe my experiences with my brothers prepared me to help Seaman. As we learn more about PTSD we discover it is more widespread than we first imagined. We also find out it has more causes that was thought in earlier days. This raised a question in my mind. Did our forefathers get the disease but did not label it as such because they did not know what it was? Or, is it really worse today because of the breakdown of the family unit? We are now being told that one of the tools for overcoming PTSD is a good support group and a loving, supportive family.

I felt that I had reached conclusion on my Seaman puzzle. But what had I concluded. I still did not have all the facts to prove Seaman had been the source of the bark-howl I had heard. Or for that matter none of the other people who had heard it, with the possible exception of the old folks in St. Louis shortly after Captain Lewis had died, had seen him when he was howling. But everyone who had heard him before me where convinced it was Seaman they had heard. Several who had heard it had also seen a large black dog close by.

I had fought from the beginning to remain objective and require facts to base my conclusions on, but I was seeing things in a bit different light.

Religious philosophies, culture based legends, other people's convictions resulting from their experiences were all piling up with facts we did have. The mixed package was a compelling argument in favor of believing Hiram and Crazy Charlie when they said it was Seaman they had heard and saw. They "knew" Seaman cured them.

What I could not overcome was the fact that the description I gave of the bark-howl I had heard that morning on the Missouri River canyon was almost the exact words that had been used by others who had heard it over the last two hundred years. I had never pondered the philosophy of reincarnation, but what research I had done brought me to the conclusion that it was possible. It had become my only answer for how the exactly same bark-howl had been heard by many people over the years.

A wild thought hit me. If a soul returns to a new life to overcome bad karma of a previous life, maybe Seaman's work to help PTSD sufferers is from a soul trying to overcome it bad karma of killing others during time of wars.

Another random thought hit me. Seaman showed himself to me down at my sister's farm. He was the one who had chased the mountain lion away just as the Nez Perces cultural legend said he had told all the animals he would do.

I recalled a comment several historians have been credited with having said or written to the idea that all the facts about historical events are impossible to find because they are not always written down or preserved for future use. The best we can hope to do is discover as much as we possibly can then postulate theories based upon sound logical conclusions using the facts we have as our basis.

Sometimes we must rely on accepting a belief or faith to fill in the void where not enough facts exist. The leap from known facts to the logical conclusion is aided by a person's beliefs. However, the great danger is to let the beliefs dictate the conclusion that cannot be logically derived. It is a very fine line that has to be walked. Probably a better secondary help is cultural oral histories. Who has the right to say that information is only fact if it is written?

I was satisfied this was the path I had trod. I concluded I, too, had heard Seaman. My job was to help him by publishing "Hiram's Notebook."

With those thoughts I declared my research on Seaman was completed. I busied myself organizing my notes so I could understand them in the event I ever wanted to access them again. To my surprise I found that I had never catalogued all the photos I had taken out on the Missouri River that fateful morning.

I started my review by deleting the duplicates, shots that did not turn out, and other ones I decided not to keep. It is a slow, time-consuming process when you are dealing with several hundred photos.

I suddenly stopped my careful study in amazement. The photo before me was a shot of a bare piece of ground on the cliffs above the river showing several animal tracks. Careful examination comparing them to wolf tracks showed them to be from a large dog. But the prints were not the normal large dog. These were somewhat fuzzy from a foot that was definitely partly webbed.

These tracks were in the sequence of photos I had taken of the area where I had heard Seaman. The date/time stamp on the photo was July 14 @ 4:08 a.m.

Bibliography

Although this is a work of fiction a considerable amount of research went into developing this story, as is typical of most books, fact or fiction.

I used the "Journals of the Lewis and Clark Expedition" edited by Dr. Gary Moulton to get the entries about Seaman as written by Captains Meriwether Lewis and William Clark. I also used these volumes for other material about Spirit Mound and the Cannonball River

For the balance of the historical record on Seaman I referred to James Holmberg's article, "Seaman's Fate" in the February 2000 issue of We Proceeded On, the quarterly journal of the Lewis and Clark Trail Heritage Foundation. That article was my source for the book written by Timothy Alden in 1814.

I used the "DeLorme Atlas and Gazetteer" for details to describe locations in central Montana, southeast Idaho, and western North Dakota.

For by discussion on tracks for wolves, coyotes, dogs, and mountain lions I referenced "Peterson's Field Guide series, Animal Tracks" written by Olaus Murie and Mark Elbroch.

These other topics I researched on a variety of internet websites. Specific sites are listed in the body of the text:

- Newfoundland dogs
- Post traumatic stress syndrome
- Animal therapy
- Animal reincarnation

Made in the USA
Middletown, DE
20 July 2023